BUM
LOVE

GEORGE ONSTOT

For W.K.

CONTENTS

i

I

Traipsing through Southlands Cemetery behind the wheezing old Ford pickup truck, Andy Kennedy told himself that dead people were no fun. The graveyard's frightening stillness unsettled him, and he felt sure he could hear chamber music coming from somewhere. Or maybe the Pope would suddenly appear, blessing everyone, even the Jews.

Andy followed the scarred truck past the cenotaphs and mausoleums and other residences of the affluent departed. Naturally, the finest ones, belonging to those who had died with the most toys, were located in the hilliest section of the cemetery so that they could spend eternity in a place with a good view and their visitors would have something to stand and gaze at while they spoke to their dear departed.

"Check that out," Andy said to Joey, his best friend for the time being. "That mausoleum? That's where Li Wong is. He owned Wong Honda, the biggest dealership in town. I used to watch his TV commercials. What a character. He must've made enough money to last a dozen lifetimes."

"That money's not doin him much good now," said Joey.

"Maybe not, but I'll bet his kids are havin a helluva nice time with it."

They continued past the Li Wong mausoleum and ended up on the humbler side of the cemetery. O'HERLIHY, RABINOWITZ, SINGH, NGUYEN read the modest gravestones. Another set of markers said KENNEDY. Andy glanced at them and looked away. He thought of his infant daughter Elisa, whom he had let slip through his fingers while trying to bathe her. They had buried her in Southlands without him, because he had run away from home.

Andy looked up and smiled at the bright sky. "Gonna be an OK day today."

"If we don't freeze to death," Joey said.

"Don't jinx us. Bayporte is the rainiest city in the world. If you get a good day, appreciate it."

"Did you know," asked Joey, "that my mum was a

Native?"

"Was not. She was a Paki or somethin. That's why you're so dark."

"My mum was a Native from Calgary. She used to work at the Stampede. She cooked hot dogs and bleached her hair."

"When I was at the Stampede," Andy said, "I never saw any blonde Native women cookin hot dogs."

"She was there. You musta missed her."

They reached their destination, two large rectangular holes in the ground that needed filling in. The coffins inside the plots gleamed with frost. The truck stopped to allow Andy and Joey to remove shovels from its bed and begin the tedious task of scooping soil from the mountain of dirt in the truck's bed and dumping it into the plots as the driver blared rock music on the radio.

Andy put down his shovel for a moment and pointed to a grave adorned with flowers and a Canadian flag. "See that one? That's Slick Willie James. He owned the Playpen, a nightclub he loved more than his own kids. I knew him when I played hockey.

He said, 'Andy, come to the Playpen whenever you want. Everything's on the house.'" He laughed. "The Playpen was just a brothel and drug store pretendin to be a nightclub."

"He was nice to invite you. Did you go?" Joey asked.

"Damn right I did." Andy laughed some more. "Slick Willie stuck his middle finger at the Establishment and got away with it. You remember when we had that woman mayor? Nancy Maloney. She walked into the Playpen one day and said, 'I want to check out this place.' So Slick Willie just happened to be in the lobby at that moment and he said, 'Sure, if you buy a ticket.' So Maloney got mad and walked out. She started sendin in the cops to get the place busted and padlocked. Slick Willie changed the Playpen's marquee to say, 'For showtimes, call Mayor Maloney's office.'"

"Did the mayor know the showtimes?" asked Joey.

Andy ignored him. "So Slick Willie mocked the mayor and laughed his ass off. After pullin stunts like that and getting death threats every week, you know what finally did him in? He got loaded and crashed his car. Cops said that if he had worn a seat belt, he might've had an open casket." Andy leaned on his shovel and shook his head. "Drinkin and drivin sure don't mix."

"This job sucks," said Joey.

Andy would never have wrecked a car while drunk. He didn't retch when he drank. He didn't smoke crack or crystal meth and had plenty of contempt for those who did. He didn't even drink cooking sherry or mouthwash. He drank low-end fortified wines like Cisco and Mad Dog. Inebriation suited him fine; it made him eloquent and contemplative. He drank until he ran out of money, and by then he had usually run out of things to say. Cheap wine didn't ravage him as it did others. He would get sleepy, sure, but gradually and agreeably so, and then he could easily find an alleyway or storefront in which to curl up and nod off. A few hours later, he would wake up, wanting more to drink—unless, of course, he'd been smart and saved some of whatever he had been imbibing before going to sleep.

But he was sober for now. He hadn't drunk anything in three or four days and guessed he felt better than all right. He had no cash, and Annie was in the middle of one of her difficult spells, so he wanted to get his shit together for her sake. Also, he needed to look his most presentable—or his least slovenly—in case he had to meet with Vince de George, the hotshot lawyer who had helped him out after he cops had busted Andy for using the ladies' washroom at the downtown police station. The lawyer had found a flaw in the arrest report and gotten the charge dropped. De George, a lifelong hockey fan who had cheered for Andy when he played for the Bullies, gave his downtrodden client a substantial discount but still insisted on being paid.

"You owe me money, Andy," he had said. "I have bills to pay. I don't work for free."

"I can't pay you money I don't have," replied Andy.

"Then get some work and make some money."

"Vince, I'm a bum. No one will hire me."

"I'll find you something." Vince de George, of course, knew many ways of making money. Later that day, the two men spoke again. "Andy, I've found you a job digging graves at Southlands Cemetery. Isn't that your old neighborhood?"

"That's on the other side of town. Do you expect me to walk all that way, then bust my ass diggin graves?"

"Come by my office and I'll leave some bus tickets with my receptionist."

Andy did as told, and de George's receptionist gave him two full booklets of transit tickets. While such items were hardly something he would have paid money for, Andy had to admit that bus tickets were a nice thing to have. So he had slept in the least decrepit part of skid row, away from the dumpsters and rats, and managed to get a decent night's rest. In the morning, he went to Saint Theresa's Mission to have coffee and look for Annie. He visited with the other indigents and wondered why Reverend Eccles kept smiling at everyone. Andy thought that Eccles needed to keep the coffee hot and his smiles to himself.

Stepping outside to smoke, Andy found a half-used Player's Light on the sidewalk and lit it with a disposable lighter he'd rescued from a trash can. He sat on the curb and sucked at the cigarette until he began to feel a nice little nicotine jolt. Then he looked up and saw Joey approach in a dark sports coat and slacks, white shirt and sturdy shoes. Joey's abundant hair was properly combed, his face shaven.

"You got a hot date tonight, guy?" Andy asked, as disheveled as ever and quite disgusted with his own stink.

Joey laughed. "No, I just got out of the hospital."

"Been in the nuthouse, eh?"

"No, the AIDS ward."

Andy smirked. "Didn't know you were queer."

"Not me. I got it from shootin dope. Doc says there's treatment for what I got, but the medicine is worse than the disease."

"Well, don't go buggerin *me*. Say, you got a few bucks?"

Joey nodded. "Yeah, enough for a cheap bottle."

"Then let's get loaded." Andy paused. "Shit, I have to work today. Wanna come along and make some money with me?"

"Doin what?"

"Diggin graves for minimum wage at Southlands Cemetery."

Joey scratched his head. "How much is minimum wage?"

"Not nearly fuckin enough."

"Southlands Cemetery? That's far away. How would we get there?"

Andy took out his booklets of bus tickets. "With these. Come on, let's go."

The two men boarded the bus for Fairview Avenue. Looking down at his shoes, which had split nearly in half, Andy felt ashamed of himself and was grateful that the driver had let him board. But the bus was warm, the seats cushioned and he was getting out of skid row for the day.

"The preacher talks a lot about the Ten Commandments," Joey said as the bus rumbled along. "'Don't murder' is one of them."

"Good advice," said Andy.

"'Don't steal' is another." Joey frowned with the effort of remembering them. "'Don't lie.'"

"Show me a man or woman that don't steal or lie," said Andy.

"Don't lust after another man's woman."

Andy laughed. "They're the best kind to lust after."

"'Don't bear false witness against your neighbor.' What does that mean?"

"I guess it means that you're not supposed to lie about your neighbor when you're testifyin in court," Andy said.

"'Don't covet.' That means you're not supposed to want what the other guy has. Right?"

"Years ago, when I played for the Bullies," Andy told him, "I had so much money and stuff that I never coveted what the other guys had."

They soon ran out of things to say. Looking out the window, Andy saw a familiar sign saying ROESKE'S HARDWARE. Gordie Roeske's father had owned that store for years, and now Gordie ran it. Andy and he had been classmates years earlier, and Andy remembered him as a fat ugly dumb Polack whose greatest aspiration in life was to run his daddy's store. Andy sighed. Gordie, the least likely kid ever to get laid or amount to anything on the playing field, and now he's got his old man's store, and what do *you* have, Andy? You have jackshit. You once were a handsome hockey stud who got more pussy than Frank Sinatra, but now you're alcoholic and homeless, shovelin graveyard dirt for chump change.

He looked across the street and saw the house he had grown up in, a small white abode he supposed his family still lived in. Well, he thought, so freakin what? let a big Bayporte storm come along and flush them all away.

Andy and Joey got off the bus directly in front of the cemetery, and Andy shivered. "Wait a minute," he said, "I gotta stretch my legs." Being back on Fairview Avenue made him anxious, with its old familiar houses and the graveyard in which some of his kin lay. Little had changed, yet everything was different. He recalled the names of his beloved hangouts up the hilly street: Triple Scoop, Pizza Guy, O Canada Records and Tapes. All gone for years, he guessed, and forgotten by everyone but him. What, he wondered, did they have up there now? Probably A Taste of India and

Bollywood Video.

"Where's that broad you usually go around with?" Joey asked. "Annie, right?"

"Annie went off to find herself."

"Maybe someone made her a better offer."

"Kinda doubt that, guy."

"But you can always get another woman, Andy."

"In a heartbeat."

"How come the women like you so much?" Joey asked.

Andy shrugged. "I must be a hell of a man."

Joey laughed. "Yeah, that's the thing that women like. You kid around a lot. You're flippant."

"What do you mean by that?"

"'Flippant' is a word I looked up on the computer in the community center."

"Guys like you shouldn't be allowed on the computer so you can look up big words to call people."

"Wasn't calling you a name. I was just makin an observation."

"Well, let's start observin some stiffs," Andy said.

They used the cemetery's front entrance and went to the small building that served as Southlands' business office. They introduced themselves to the lady in the office, who told them where to go. Minutes later, they began shoveling dirt and Andy talked about Slick Willie.

"You know what really bugs me?" Joey asked.

"Lots of things bug *me*," Andy said.

"Well, what bugs me right now is this: if you die and don't have a headstone, how's anyone ever gonna know you had lived?"

"If you're dead," Andy replied, "what fuckin difference does it make?"

He thought some more about Li Wong.

The car dealer had appeared each weeknight on TV, a goofy little guy beaming and clowning around in those insipid little ads. "Come see me soon! I make you best deal in town on Honda! You hear me?" Andy assumed that Wong Honda's gigantic neon sign still lit up much of King Street near the behemoth shopping mall they had cleverly named Bay Porte. He hated that mall as much as he hated the light-rail system,

FasTrain, where the transit cops eyed him as if at any moment they expected him to haul out his dingus and waved it at everyone.

Wong's mausoleum reminded him of something, and he grew frustrated as he pondered the matter. Perhaps it made him think of the TV documentaries of the Parthenon, King Tut's tomb or the Taj Mahal. Why did these eminent rich people insist on having their remains stored in such grandiose, expensive edifices? Did it make them believe, as Andy suspected, that they were somehow cheating death?

To Andy, the Wong mausoleum looked spacious enough to accommodate half of Hong Kong, and that was part of the thing bugging him. Wong had all that space for his withered old bones, and yet so many of Andy's dead friends didn't even get a decent grave and marker. He thought of his pugilist friend Johnny Goodtimes, a silver medalist in the 1984 Los Angeles Olympics. After Andy's daughter died and he took off, he met up with Johnny Goodtimes, who by then had degenerated into drunkenness and vagrancy.

The two men bummed across Canada. On their

way home, they slept in the wilderness and, one morning, Johnny clutched his chest and fell over, dead. Andy remembered it as a magnificent spring morning and was about to suggest to Johnny that they remain in the wilderness for a day or two longer. Instead, he looked down at his dead friend and said, *Well, Johnny, I'm gonna leave you here to be lunch for the wolves. They'll enjoy every bite of you, and you'll be doin the world a favor by bein food for hungry wildlife, and I think that's somethin you should be proud of.*

Andy went back to Bayporte alone. He considered people's fears and obsessions with death just so much nonsense. He wouldn't mind, after he croaked, if they just threw him to the wolves or dumped him into the sea for the sharks. He wouldn't even mind if he ended up on a cold steel table, being cut up by medical students. Just so long as they don't stand around laughin at my shriveled-up old pecker.

"Are you from around here?" Joey asked as they kept shoveling dirt. "You seem familiar with the area."

"Used to be."

"Do you miss it?"

"I miss bein young and handsome." Andy glanced over his shoulder, to where he knew his family members were buried. They had bought several plots side by side, but a few Kennedys had perished soon rather than later, so Andy wasn't sure that they had saved a plot for him, if he wanted it.

They had buried James Kennedy under a dazzling sun. James, Andy's father, now lay about a dozen meters from where Andy now stood. Normally stoical, Andy had been convulsed with grief as he stood among the other mourners, for he had witnessed his father's death and could not escape its dreadful visions even in sleep. Jimmy Kennedy, hustling across Fairview Avenue in the middle of a torrent of nighttime rain, had failed to elude a speeding sedan; his severed right leg bounced across the darkened, drenched street like a meaty limb thrown to hungry dogs. Fairview Avenue soon became clogged with emergency vehicles whose flashing lights illuminated the entire block. The dead man's blood colored the roadway for half the night.

Andy, horrified, had watched the incident from his

family's living room window, which looked out directly over Fairview Avenue. Jimmy, blessed with many friends and admirers, looked handsome even in his casket as his countless admirers wept. In his obituary, he received praise as a spirited singer, efficient manager and true *mensch*. Great Elizabeth Flour, his employer, gave everyone the morning off to say goodbye. Then Mum ruled the Kennedy household until, some years later, she joined her husband in Southlands. Maybe there's a plot for me too, Andy thought. But it would be too close to Mum. She'd rag on me from six feet under.

"This is a nice place," Joey said. "For a boneyard."

"Nothin nice about a boneyard."

Andy found his daughter's grave and soon stood before it. He remembered the moment when Elisa had slipped through his fingers and drowned in the bathwater. He wished to be transported back to that moment just before bathing his child so that he could throw himself into the Tyson River and spare Elisa's life. But his wish did not come true and he remained there at his daughter's grave. He wept profusely and wiped away his tears as he cleared his throat. He spoke to his dead child's headstone.

"I remember it all, no matter how I try to forget. I wasn't drinkin much, so I can't blame the booze. Tom knew right away what happened. He said, 'Why is the baby blue?' He's been a good son to me. He's gotten me out of trouble a few times and even slipped me some cash. Fighting back more tears, he just nodded and skulked away.

"Let's get goin," he said to Joey.

"You know someone here?"

"Yeah. Little girl."

"How'd she die?" he asked.

"Pissed her pants."

"Died from pissin her pants?" Joey asked. "Hell, I piss my pants all the time, and look at me."

"Yeah," said Andy. "Look at you."

II

Andy and Joey boarded the bus and headed back to skid row. Andy reminded himself again to thank Vince de George for the bus tickets. Whenever anyone does you a favor, remember to thank em, because you never know when you'll need to ask for another favor.

"Andy," Joey asked, "where are we goin now?"

"What's it to ya?"

Joey shrugged. "Just like to know where I'm goin."

"You're nowhere, on your way to no place." He paused. "We're goin to the mission, to see if Annie's there."

Joey nodded. "Good idea. We can eat there, too. It's a decent meal he gives you."

"Is not. I've eaten better out of dumpsters," Andy said.

"At least it's free."

"Wrong again. You have to sit there and listen to him preach till he'll let you eat. 'Turn your life over to

Jesus and get a fresh, shiny new start. You'll become happy and handsome and a delight to your friends.' He's just blowin sunshine up your ass. He says this to a bunch of old losers like me who don't want new souls, just a warm place to sit and a meal to eat."

"I believe what the preacher says," Joey told him. "I am a Christian."

"Yeah? Then how come He lets you rot in skid row?"

"There is a reason for all things."

They stared out the window as the bus rolled along Broadway Street. As a Bullies forward years earlier, Andy had prowled the city's many nightclubs, his pockets bursting with cash, his face known to all. He thought now of those darkened lounges and pretty women who told him he looked like Jack Nicholson. The managers and bartenders wanted only to shake his hand and pour him free drinks. The dope dealers sauntered by to pay their respects and offer him a taste.

"When I played for the Bullies," Andy told Joey, "every man wanted to know me and every woman wanted to blow me." Then he wondered why he'd said it. Andy hadn't yet made up his mind about this new guy. Joey, naïve and gullible, vulnerable and forgetful, clung to him like a whimpering puppy. Garrulous and self-pitying, Joey often complained about his dreadful, doomed existence and succumbed to spectacular, endless crying jags.

Andy, with very few friends left, empathized with Joey's desire for brotherhood and camaraderie., and at times truly admired Joey's willingness to play the pathetic, losing hand that life had dealt him. Often, Andy felt that he and Joey were travelers stranded in an unfamiliar train station, stuck with each other, bound for nowhere. They also shared a belief in remaining men together, in salvaging whatever dignity remained for two indigent, aging males whom society regarded with mockery and contempt. Andy, far more functional and lucid than most other comparably disenfranchised people, secretly believed in a hierarchy of the homeless, as absurdly oxymoronic as such a thing sounded. He prided himself on his knowledge of the etiquette, protocols and taboos of the marginalized. He and Joey hated rain, rats, cops and Jesus freaks. They liked premium liquor, friendly dogs and sexy women. Me and Joey, he thought. We're the best of the worst. Top of the bottom.

He closed his eyes, rested his chin on his chest and let his mind wander back to 1992. Long after his retirement from the Bullies, his team, through luck as much as anything else, played the Boston Bruins in the Stanley Cup Finals. The Bullies, after losing the first three games, clawed their way back to force game seven in Beantown. In Bayporte, hockey fans packed into downtown pubs to watch the game on huge TVs.

After their team gave up a heartbreaking goal in overtime, surly men in Bullies apparel emerged from the pubs and lingered downtown, gumming up traffic. Vastly outnumbered, the police just stood by their cruisers and wagons. Some kid climbed a streetlight and, like a circus performer, walked along the overhead bus cables as the crowd cheered him on. Mosh pits formed; fistfights started but soon ended. A second kid climbed a streetlight, kicked apart a Starbucks sign and pumped his fist as the cops on the sidewalk gestured for him to come down.

On the sidewalk nearby stood Andy Kennedy, anonymous and grubby. A few feet away, a girl fainted, and Andy just watched her collapsed. A cop pushed his way towards her, reached her and shouted for everyone to back off. Nobody did, so he took out a small black canister and blasted them and Andy, with pepper spray. Enraged, Andy wiped at his eyes and groped in his pocket for the fist-sized rock he carried for protection. With gnashing teeth, gripped the rock, reared back and slammed it into the cop's face.

The cop fell face first, his blood gushing onto the people he had just sprayed. Pushing through the crowd, his heart hammering in his ears, Andy fled from the cops who were now surely chasing him.

Ron Porter, the bludgeoned cop, had been in his late twenties, a lifelong Bayporter who had studied criminal justice at a local community college. He now appeared in Andy's dream, his face disfigured by that rock.

Why did you kill me?

Why did you spray me with that pepper shit? I was

just retaliatin.

You hit me in the face with that rock and I dropped dead.

You were an officer of the law who mishandled a situation. You didn't know how to do your job.

I needed to help someone who had fainted and you people wouldn't step back. I had no other options.

Well, neither did I. If you hadn't sprayed me, you might still be alive.

Oh? And when have you done your job right? You've rarely failed to fail. How long has it been since you ran away from your family? Have you thought about that lately?

My family is none of your bloody business. After I drowned my kid, I couldn't cope with things, so I left.

Poor baby. You just ran off like a coward.

"If you're gonna pick on me, just fuck off!"

"I'm not pickin on you," said Joey.

Andy blinked, looked around and collected himself. "Do you remember that riot a few years back?"

"After the Bullies lost in the finals?" Joey asked. "Yeah, I remember it. Were you in it?"

Andy smirked. "I kinda *started* it."

"A cop got killed that day," Joey recalled. "They're

still lookin for the guy that did it."

"Well, they haven't been lookin hard enough. That guy's still around." Andy thought for a moment. "I was just dreamin about it. After that cop dropped dead, I ran off and went into my favorite hidin places in case they came lookin for me. Then I snuck over to the train station so I could get out of town. I climbed into a boxcar goin east, and a couple of other guys wanted in, too. But the bloody boxcar started movin, and the cops come runnin up and started shootin! Them fuckin scumbags! Well, the first guy got in OK, but the second guy didn't. So the one who got in, once he could catch his breath, said, 'There was a riot goin on in town just now. I heard some guy killed a cop. That's life in prison.'"

The man Andy had tried to save, Marco Rigoni, had emigrated from Italy in search of moneymaking opportunities. He decided that drugs and prostitution involved too much danger, so he resorted to shoplifting. Andy wondered why the cops had shot him over something as trivial as bumming a ride on a train.

Rigoni boarded the bus now and approached Andy with a smile and extended his hand.

"I don't shake hands with shoplifters," said Andy.

"I'm no shoplifter, just a bum," said Joey.

"And proud of it," said Andy.

Their bus soon reached skid row and the two bums got off. Andy, once again struck by the coldness of the day, wondered how much longer he could go on; how many more cold days and colder nights would he have to endure?

In the alley next to Saint Theresa's Mission, an old woman sat propped up against the building like a child's doll. Her gray hair poked out in tufts from beneath her soiled hoodie. Her sweatpants and sneakers looked almost as bad as Andy's clothes.

"That's Flo," Andy said. "Not sure why she's just sittin there like that."

"Just sleepin it off," said Joey. "You know her, eh?"

Andy nodded. "She's been workin the streets for years. She moved down here from Yukon or the Northwest Territories."

Joey moved in a bit closer. "Not sure if she's still

alive."

Andy moved in closer, too. "Still breathin, but she better get up before the rats eat her." He bent double at the waist and moved in till his face and hers were just a few centimeters apart. "Flo? It's me, Andy."

She opened one eye the tiniest bit. "Undee?"

He straightened up and shook his head. "Pissed out of her tree. If she just sits there, the rats'll get her. Or Jack Frost will get her, then the rats'll eat her." He took a breath. "She needs to go inside the mission, but the preacher won't let drunks in. He don't believe in helpin them that need it most." Then, "Flo? You want somethin to eat?"

"Hey?"

"You want some food?"

"Wanna drinka rum."

Andy rubbed his stomach. "Food yum."

"Rum yum."

Any went into the mission and saw Reverend Eccles standing at the lectern. The preacher's deep voice filled the overheated room. His audience consisted of some dozing men in folding chairs. A tall, spare man with graying hair and small eyes magnified by glasses with pop-bottle lenses, Eccles seemed to be staring at the one woman in his audience.

Andy smiled.

Annie.

Saint Theresa's Mission, she insisted, had become nothing but a boys' club. The women's shelter had better food and fewer weirdos, but she always went to Saint Terry's instead. Her beige toque, always pulled over her eyes and ears like a mop-top hairdo, made her look like the Beatles' broken-down sister. Crossing her arms and legs, she cocked her head at Eccles as if she were a cynical juror sitting through a lawyer's argument.

Keep it up, preacher, Andy thought from the back of the room. Raising his arm to scratch his itchy chin, he could scarcely believe how foul his body odor had become.

"Jesus is the way!" Eccles shouted. A practical man, he used his battered copy of the New Testament mainly as a prop and relied on what he considered straight talk, as if he were speaking as Jesus Himself, in

His white, white robe. Eccles sought to help those he could. The most unfortunate of them—the righteous dopefiends who would relapse a dozen times or more before overcoming their addictions, if their day ever came—were welcome to come in for a meal and an hour out of the cold, but nothing more.

"Jesus is everywhere," Eccles told his audience. "But so is Satan. It is the eternal battle. Jesus endured the crucifixion in order to save our souls. His death meant everlasting life for those who deserve it, and each of you can be born again, right here and now, if you will accept Him as your lord and savior. Will you? *Will you?*"

His audience just sat there, offering him little grunts and nods. From the kitchen came the sound of clattering dishes and the unmistakable smell of dinner.

"Then amen to you, too," said Eccles as he walked away.

"I thought he'd never leave," Andy muttered as he and the others ambled over to the table where the volunteers dispensed the meals. He found Big Red and said, "Red, Flo's freezin out there. Can't you do somethin for her?"

Big Red Robinson, a recovering alcoholic with a headful of fire-colored hair unmuted by age, managed the mission for Eccles. He shook his head. "Reverend personally kicked her out. She was so bloody tight that he thought she would puke on him."

"Well, can't I at least sneak her a cup of soup or somethin?" Andy asked.

Big Red shrugged. "OK, but to tell you the truth, the soup is awfully thin today. Let me see if I can get her something more substantial." He went into the kitchen and came back with a small bowl of applesauce. "I don't know if she'll eat it, but you can give it to her anyway."

Andy nodded. "Better than nothin." He and Joey went outside and got Flo to sit up straight against the building. Andy spooned out a small mouthful of the yellowish mush and held it to her lips. "Eat."

"Rum?"

"No rum. Just applesauce."

"Want rum."

"Did you know," Joey said, "that Flo once studied

to become a nun?"

"That right, eh?" Andy asked Flo, "Did you really?"

"Yeah. Nun." She grimaced. "Yuck."

"So," Andy asked, "what stopped you from becomin a nun?"

"Drinkin and screwin."

She finished the applesauce and Andy returned the bowl to Big Red, who asked, "She gonna make it?"

"Probably not." Andy went into the washroom and washed his hands. Then he did the best he could to finger-comb his hair, wishing that he had some deodorant and fresh clothes. Then he joined Annie, who sat sipping tea with Joey.

"Long time, no see, darlin."

"Not long enough." She didn't look at him.

"Where did you spend last night?"

"Why do you ask?" Annie just stared straight ahead.

"Tell me. I wanna know. I did some work today."

"Really?" she asked with false cheer, staring at her tea cup. "Who did you rob?"

"You're funny. I worked outside all day and made some money."

"Doing what?"

"Manual labor. Manly work."

She turned to him ad fixed him with her big brown eyes. "Seriously?"

He grinned. "Would I bullshit you?"

"How goes it, Annie?"

They looked up and saw Reverend Eccles.

"Fine, just fine." She showed Eccles what Andy recognized as that mean little smile she displayed whenever she felt patronized, which was most of the time.

"Nice to hear. Andy, I think I have some work for you."

"I worked today, you know."

Eccles nodded. "That's a fine start, but I think I have something better in mind. Pawlowski, a local philanthropist, is getting on in years and needs a helper for when he picks up donations in his truck. Interested?"

Andy shrugged. "Maybe."

"He's waiting to hear from you."

"I'll call him tomorrow. Maybe he has a pair of

socks I could borrow. Mine are dissolvin."

Eccles smiled. "I can help you with *that* right now. I have a Christmas box left over. Let me go get it."

As soon as Eccles left, Annie muttered, "That preacher—"

"Don't be a bitch," Andy muttered back. "He's goin to get me some socks."

"We gettin a bottle tonight" Joey asked.

"Andy, I hope you're not drinking," Annie said.

Andy shook his head. "No drinkin,"

"If we have money," Annie said, "we can get our suitcases back and get a room for the week."

"I owe the lawyer some money," Andy said. "I have to put aside some for him." He leaned in closer to Annie. "So, sweetness, where did you sleep last night?"

"Where did *you* sleep, Andy?" she retorted.

"Oh, I found a cozy little hole to crawl into. Did you sleep in Boylan's tent?"

She shuddered. "No I did not."

"So where then?"

"I slept at Dan and Bev's."

Andy arched an eyebrow. "But you don't like them."

"It was either sleep at their place or sleep outside and get hypothermia."

"I think," he said, "that you made the right choice."

Big Red came over with a cup of coffee and joined them. He had spent years as the head chef at Panache, Bayporte's premier restaurant. *The New York Times* had written about Big Red's cooking with praise and the *Michelin Guide* had done so without insult. His social life had included Hollywood stars who owned homes in Bayporte and came to Panache for salmon steaks and white wine. After a few too many parties and far too many false friends, Big Red woke up divorced, drunk and depressed. At Eccles' insistence, he entered a rehabilitation program and later became the manager of Saint Theresa's Mission, where he boasted of his former culinary glory to, and lorded over, the mission's kitchen staff.

Andy, during his NHL career, had gone on drinking binges with Big Red. After Big Red became sober, Andy stayed drunk, drifting in and out of town.

He had been back in Bayporte only a few months when, in desperation, he entered the downtown police detachment and asked to use the men's washroom. The receptionist, sitting behind four inches of bullet-proof glass, refused to give him the key because he didn't have an appointment with anyone in the building. When he emphasized how badly he needed to use their toilet, she told him that his bursting bowels were *his* problem, not theirs. Andy walked away, but as he passed the ladies' room, its door swung open and someone exited, and Andy slipped inside before the door closed. As he darted into a stall, one or two men screamed, and soon a woman constable rushed in. she tapped on the stall door as Andy sat, pants down, eyes closed in mute gratitude, face and clothes drenched in sweat. He emerged, nearly half an hour later, docile as a Hindu cow, as the officer handcuffed him.

His lawyer, Vince de George, had gotten the charges dropped for reasons Andy had never completely understood nor particularly cared about. A social worker referred him to Saint Theresa's Mission, and there he met up again with Big Red. Andy still liked hi, of course, but the ribald wit of Panache seemed so much different now—serious, somber, *sober*—that Andy wondered: Was the new Red really such an improvement over the old one?

"You'll never guess," Big Red was saying now, "who's working at the Abyss."

"You're right," Andy replied, "we'll never guess. Tell us."

Big Red grinned. "Kelly Wadham."

Andy cackled. "Really? What's he doin?"

"Tending bar."

Annie's mouth dropped open. "Kelly Wadham, who had all those hit records back in the 'Seventies?"

Big Red nodded. "Andy and I knew him well."

"He was quite the big star," Annie said, "and not just here in Canada. They liked him all over the world. What happened to him?"

Big Red shrugged. "The usual: Drugs, women, divorces, lawsuits."

Annie smiled. "I used to sing some of his songs."

"I didn't know you could sing," said Big Red.

"I certainly can. I can play piano, too. I studied

music at Julliard, in New York City. When my father died, I had to drop out and come back home."

"I went to Julliard," interjected Joey. "I was there for two hours. I had lunch and bought a T-shirt."

Annie rolled her eyes. "It *is* a first-rate school."

Andy said, "Let's go see Kelly."

"Let's not and say we did," quipped Big Red.

"You think I'd get drunk?" asked Andy.

"Yes," Big Red and Annie answered together.

"I don't go into bars anymore," Big Red added.

"Couldn't we just drop by, have a pop and say hi?" Andy asked, nearly whining. "Come on, it'll be fun to see Kelly again. At least he's still alive and kickin, and I don't have that many friends left."

Just then, Eccles returned with a gift-wrapped box that looked like something from the Christmas issue of a ladies' magazine—peach-colored, silky, perfumed. "Here you be, Andy."

"Uh, thanks." Andy accepted the gift box, his grizzled cheeks darkening with a blush as deep as the package's pink bow. The gift boxes, handed out by police officers to street people as the P.D.'s public relations department stood by with video cameras, came in blue for men and peach for women.

Big Red laughed. "Reverend, I think that one was meant for someone else."

"Hey," Andy blurted, "I don't give a shit if there's Tampax and lipsticks in here. I just want some new socks." He tore off the wrapping paper, crushed it into a greasy ball and tossed it aside. Inside the box were two pairs of polyester socks, one package of Player's Lights cigarettes and two candy bars. "Thanks, Reverend," Andy said, "these oughta last me a while." He stuck the candy, cigarettes and one pair of socks into his pocket.

The mission's door opened and a short, chubby young man came in wearing a mackinaw and stood there for several moments, as if wondering what to do next.

"Clark!" shouted Big Red. "Close the bloody door! You're letting the cold air in!"

Clark frowned, as if Big Red had spoken to him in a foreign language he had just begun learning.

"He's hopeless," said Big Red, shaking his head.

Reverend Eccles confronted Clark. "Your pupils are huge. You're high as a kite. Where did you get the money for drugs?"

"Friend lent me money," Clark muttered.

"You have no friends. You're a liar and a thief. Leave immediately. Brendan, get his suitcase."

Big Red nodded and went upstairs, to the row of bedrooms in which the residents slept as they resolved to begin life anew. Eccles had repeatedly invited Andy to move in, where he would have a narrow room with a single bed, dresser and Bible, and three starchy meals per day while he answered the question, "How can I make today better than yesterday?" The residents lived under an injunction to stay off drugs, do their chores and make specific plans for self-reliance.

Big Red came back down with Clark's suitcase. "Goodbye and good luck."

"Give us a fag, Red," said Clark.

"I quit smoking years ago."

"I've got some in my suitcase. Let me get them out."

"Clark," Eccles said, "you must go now."

"I got nowhere to go."

"Go stay with the friend who lent you the money for drugs."

"What about my suitcase? All my crap is in there."

"Then leave it here. Your property will be safe. Go out into the night and decide if you want to stay drunk or begin a sober new life. Come back tomorrow if you're sober. Your suitcase will still be here."

Clark scratched his head and made a face like a petulant child. "I want my cigs."

"Then get them and get out."

Clark, moving as if underwater, opened his suitcase and got his cigarettes. As he floated out the door, he said, "Don't miss me too much."

...

Andy smiled. Soft, dry socks with firm elastic felt so good. What a difference a small thing could make, he said to himself as he led Joey, Annie and Big Red out of the mission. In the alley, Flo remained motionless.

"Red," Andy said, "you got a blanket or somethin for her?"

"I'll go look."

Over the years, Andy had watched many people drift off into the solemn nonsense of death. Here one moment, gone the next, probably better off on the other side, if there was another side.

"Wonder whose ass we could kiss," Andy said, "to get an ambulance over here and get Flo admitted to the hospital so she don't freeze to death."

"The ambulance wouldn't come," Annie said, "and if it did, the doctors at the hospital might keep her overnight for observation, but that's all. They might give her a referral to rehab and put her back out on the street. I'm sure she's been through all that a few times already."

Andy looked down at Flo. "She won't last the night out here."

"Unnnnnn."

"You say somethin, Flo?"

"Rummmm."

"She wants rum," Annie said.

"Wouldn't mind a little drinkie-poo myself," Andy muttered.

Big Red came back out with a shapeless, frayed

item that once had been a gray blanket. "Best I can do."

"Good enough." Andy wrapped the blanket around Flo. "Come on, let's go. Can't do anythin more."

As they walked down the street, Andy asked Big Red, "When Flo was workin, did you ever make it with her?"

"I did when she was worth the time, trouble and expense. She really was a decent-lookin woman. Then her old man split and she tried to drink herself to death. The demand for her services kind of declined after that."

"Heartbreak," said Annie, "has ruined many a beautiful woman."

"Age and booze," retorted Andy, "have ruined many a beautiful man."

"Heartbreak is the worst. It is the worst thing that can happen to a woman."

"A hangover is the worst thing that can happen to a man." Andy turned to Big Red. "Just where the hell are we goin?"

"We're goin to see Kelly Wadham at the Abyss."

"Never heard of it. These skid row dumps used to be my favorite places when I was a kid. I would go in, get pissed and let the strippers shake their titties in my face."

"Andy," Annie admonished, "there's a lady present. Be a gentleman."

"I *am* bein a gentleman. I should be on the cover of *Gentlemen's Quarterly*." He looked up and said, "Check out that sky. Gotta be a zillion stars up there. Moon's hangin so low, I bet I could just reach up and touch it."

Annie slipped her arm through Andy's. "It's so cold, but it's lovely. Don't you think so?"

Andy nodded. "Cold but lovely. A wonderful night."

...

The sign said ABYSS in lurid red-neon script. Inside, the place looked much like its name: vast and dark, with many tables and a huge dance floor. Signs overhead said MUST BE 19 OR OLDER, GOVT ID REQUIRED. Another one said STUDENTS ALWAYS ½ OFF. Throughout the Abyss, video screen glared with the image of a famous, leather-clad blonde woman writhing to a monotonous beat, her voice Auto Tuned and scarcely audible above the din of conversation.

Step into the Abyss, Andy told himself. You've been in it for years. You just didn't know they had a name for it.

Annie looked up at the video screen and sneered at the blonde bimbo licking her lips and spreading her legs. "Do they call that call that entertainment?"

"They call that tits and ass," said Andy. They stepped up to the bar and he looked around at the other customers scattered about. Whores, pimps, queers, con men, parolees, psychotics and sons of bitches. Behind the bar, a handsome man in a white shirt looked at them and smiled. "May I help you?"

Big Red and Annie ordered Cokes and Joey asked for a gin and tonic.

"I'll have a pint of Diefenbaker's," Andy said.

Annie glared at him. "I thought you said you weren't drinking."

He smiled. "I lied."

As the bartender served them, Andy fixed him with such a brazen smile that he frowned and looked over at Big Red, who regarded him with a huge smirk.

"Is my fly open or something?" the man asked.

"You look like someone I used to get in trouble with," said Andy.

The bartender smiled back. "I think I remember you now." He ran a hand through his graying blond hair. "You got me drunk a few hundred times."

"Just a few hundred." He extended his hand. "Kelly Wadham, I'm Andy Kennedy. This here's my old lady, Annie, who's hangin out with me till Mr. Right comes along."

"Big Red Robinson," said Big Red, shaking Kelly's hand.

"I remember you from Panache," Kelly told him.

"Good memory."

"This here's my pal Joey," said Andy. "He don't got a last name. He sold it for a bottle of Canadian Comfort."

Kelly shook Joey's hand. "Good man." Then, "Well, I'm Kelly Wadham, old and bold but still not cold. And I quit drinking years ago."

Andy tugged at his filthy coat. "You like this? I hear the grunge look is comin back."

"Hey," replied Kelly, "you're better dressed than some of the Northup University kids who come here on the weekends."

"Street people, college kids…we're all the same," said Andy.

"The only difference," Kelly told him, "is that street people have already forgotten more than college kids have ever learned."

Andy nodded.

"Kelly, do you still sing?" Annie asked.

"Once in a while. Want to see one of my old videos?"

"Anything would be better than that idiot girl on the screen right now."

Kelly turned around and tapped on the computer screen. The blonde bimbo instantly disappeared. Andy smiled, hearing the first notes of a Wadham song. He looked up at the screen and saw the image of his old friend as a much younger man. He pointed at all the knobs and buttons Kelly had just used. "High tech comes to skid row, hey?"

"We need the fancy equipment for karaoke nights. We have every video you can think of. The kids from college come here every weekend to drink cheap beer and make assholes of themselves."

Andy laughed. "Well, if you wanna make an asshole of yourself, karaoke is the way to do it."

"*Run Away*," said Annie. "I haven't heard that song in years. In my crowd, it wasn't hip to like you or Billy Joel or Elton John, but I liked you anyway."

"I'm so flattered."

They all fell silent and watched the video of the artist as a young man, strumming his six-string guitar on stage. Kelly Wadham, not much past the legal drinking age, already a famous musician, his name blazing six feet tall on marquees in New York City, Toronto, London, Tokyo. Tireless, razor-thin and punked out in studded leathers, blond hair brush cut, face fashionably pockmarked. Andy, whose interest in popular culture seldom went beyond the Bayporte Bullies, recalled an inebriated evening with Kelly at

Roy's on Royal, Bayporte's most popular nightclub when both men were in their prime. Kelly, high on Canadian Comfort, climbed onto the temporarily vacant stage and serenaded the house a cappella.

In the audience, Andy admired his friend's fine tenor voice and the delight he gave to the whistling, cheering crowd. Andy supposed that even now, Kelly, just an aging, anonymous bartender, could probably outperform most of the pretty boys who attracted standing-room-only crowds and sold thousands of downloaded songs each minute on iTunes.

Alas, Andy knows that Kelly has become a mere footnote in Canadian musical history; he and his music are old and exhausted; they have lost whatever relevance they may have had.

Andy wants to complain to Kelly about the two of them. Two remarkably talented men, subjected to life's most dramatic ups and downs, men who have suffered so much—so much!—in their journeys through this world. What, he wants to know, have they received in return? A reunion in the Abyss? Is that all? Andy wants to ask: What happened to you, Kelly? What brought you down? Booze didn't do me in, though everyone thinks it did. Not even drownin my kind destroyed me. Mum and Dad drove me crazy for all those years, so I would love to hang it all on them, but that wouldn't be accurate, either. What went wrong for us, Kelly, and how come nobody ever came along to help us put things right?

The first Wadham video ended and the second one began. Kelly looked the same in both: stunningly confident, irresistibly exuberant. The worthlessness of this man's past to his present mystified Andy. How, he asked himself, could anyone be that good and still end up in a shithouse like the Abyss?

He thought back to his years with the Bullies. With the instincts of a greyhound chasing a rabbit, he had spent countless hours pursuing wayward pucks in rinks all over North America, upending smaller players and outmaneuvering bigger ones, deking left and right, and with the deftest flick of the wrist, flipping the puck past the sprawling goalie. *He shoots! He scores!*

Annie, swaying to the Kelly Wadham song as she sipped her Coke, leaned over and kissed Andy on the lips. He tingled with embarrassment. He considered her an adequate lay at best, no worse than many and better than quite a few, and he'd had hundreds of them over the years in a dozen cities. At *his* best, he remained as virile and carnal as the next middle-aged, hard-drinking man.

"Andy just can't do enough for me," Annie said as the video ended. "When he had money, he naturally wanted to spend it on me. He didn't care about rent, food and other necessities. What mattered to him was that I got my flowers or gold chain or whatever he thought would make me happy. Isn't that right, sweetie?"

He nodded. "Always." He had no idea what she was talking about.

"Lovers in love." Kelly smiled at the bragging bag lady.

"Indeed," she said with a dreamy sigh. "We kept an apartment together near West Shore. Two thousand square feet with a big balcony. Renovated by a top designer. We had everything we needed, didn't we, hon?"

"Everythin." Andy didn't know anything about West Shore apartments.

"We indulged in every way. We ate so many gourmet meals that we nearly joined Jenny Craig."

"When was all this?" Big Red asked. "I don't remember Andy ever staying in town for that long."

Andy shrugged. "Don't ask me. My memory isn't that good. I was drinkin a lot back then."

"Yes," Annie said. "Andy was drinking too much. He just couldn't stay sober, and we lost our beautiful things. I had to pawn my gold to pay our bills. I had to stop buying music and instruments. I had a lovely grand piano that I would play every day."

Andy nodded. "I remember that piano. She can sing like a bloody angel, too."

"Then sing for us," Kelly said.

"When?"

"How about right now?"

"Really?"

"Absolutely. Name your tune."

"*Imagine.* The Joan Baez version." Then, "No. I want to sing something just for Andy. One of your songs. *In Your Arms.*"

Kelly nodded and tapped on his computer screen. Then he grabbed a cordless microphone sitting in a dock next to the computer and walked Annie to the rear of the dance floor.

"Ladies and gentlemen, allow me to present the lovely and talented Miz Annie Fenberg." He handed her the microphone and hustled back to the bar.

Fondling the microphone in that way performers have—and Miz Fenberg wants these people to know that she *is* a performer, even if she does not especially look like one—she raises the microphone to her lips and pretends for a naughty instant that it's an ebony phallus, like the one she saw on screen that evening Andy took her to the Venus Theatre. The Penis Theatre, he called it. She lets the melody wash all over her, all melodies can do that for her—make her feel joy, allow her to remember the everyday miracles of friendship and loyalty. Songs from her youth in the 'Sixties and 'Seventies, songs about family and country and nature, timeless values everyone should embrace. How music could speak to her in ways that other people could not! Of love and laughter, sky and earth, rebirth and redemption. Music, Annie's closest friend all her life, has spoken of love to her, not just as notes and chords but in human terms, like a confidante's trusted voice.

Her performance this evening, such as it was, made her heart pound and pulse race. She belonged on the stage an longed to return to it. Music: the language of her life, the only thing she had ever really cared about and the only profession to which she had ever aspired.

Spotting Andy at the bar, she felt overwhelming empathy for him, this man who had been with her for so long now, who had come to know her so well after she had long ago stopped being someone worth knowing, just as she had quite obviously missed the best of him. Now they needed to be grateful for their time together because both were getting older and sicker. Annie, like Andy, believed that very little remained of her essential value. Her lovers, like his, had been not so few, and hardly far in between. Her first man had a passion that frightened her. But ultimately he surrendered her to her next man, and soon Annie grew convinced that her boyfriends willingly gave her up because they considered her too much trouble to have around. By the time she met Andy, she had become known behind her back as Annoying Annie, eternal recidivist at the crime of self-destructive relationships. Always in love with love.

At the Abyss now, after a lifetimes of learning to sing the blues, Annie won't deny her ambivalence about this return to the stage. This crowd in the Abyss—*this abyss*—is nor what she had in mind. She does not know how she will sound, since she hasn't sung in years, not even warmup exercises. Wearing a tattered black coat that she's worn for God only knows how long, she faces her audience with a queer sort of pride and pushes back her toque, a gesture meant to convey a stylish indifference to style.

Her crowd welcomes her with some halfhearted applause and she hears the beginning of *In Your Arms*. Knowing that these people aren't altogether eager to hear her sing, she thinks: Too bloody bad—it's *my* night.

Andy watches and listens, can tell that she's no

good anymore, her voice is gone and it's doubtful she could ever get it back, so he just stands and watches. You went to Julliard, kiddo, and might've been headed for the big time that you said you didn't want. Others, with inferior looks and talent, went fast and far, while you stood still and then went backwards. But don't feel too bad. You saw what happened to Janis Joplin, Whitney Houston and Amy Winehouse. And what about that little chippie that was on the video screen when we first come in this dump. How long you think *she's* gonna last at the top? She's as fake as her silicone tits, she'll be gone and forgotten soon enough, and good riddance, too. But Annie Fenberg is still around and singin again, if not altogether too good.

She ends her performance to another smattering of applause, and her audience goes back to talking and drinking. Back at the bar, she returns the microphone to Kelly. Andy pecks her on the forehead and says, "Very nice, old gal."

"Thanks for that," Kelly says.

"You're so welcome," Annie says. "I'd love to come back and do it again. Performing is my life."

III

Joey wandered off to find an alleyway to hole up and sleep in. Andy and Annie walked Big Red back to the mission. Andy had spent most of his money at the Abyss, and Kelly served them several free rounds, drawing frowns from Annie. But Andy, for the moment, seemed to be in a good mood, and Annie didn't want to make him mad. The three of them took their time walking, because Annie was notoriously slow.

"You doin OK, old gal?" Andy threw an arm around her. "City's quiet, eh? All tucked in for the night."

Annie looked skyward. "There's not a cloud up there. All the stars are out. If it wasn't freezing and we weren't homeless—"

"Then we'd really have it made." He laughed. They reached the mission and turned into the alley, find Flo just as they had left her. Big Red checked her out and shook his head. "She's gone. I better go inside and call nine-one-one."

"At least the rats didn't get her," Andy said. "Red, let's you and me carry her into the mission till the coroner gets here."

"You two got a place to spend the night?" he asked. "You're welcome to stay in the mission, if you don't mind those hard benches."

"No thanks," said Annie. "I'll stay with Dan and Bev again."

"I'll walk you over there," Andy said. "It'll give me a chance to figure out where *I'm* gonna stay."

. . .

After saying goodnight to Big Red, they headed up Grand Street, in the general direction of Dan and Bev's condominium near Pioneer Park. Andy, more or less a lifelong resident of Bayporte, surveyed Grand Street as the two walked along. The street had changed far more than he ever could have imagined or desired. Its last mom-and-pop shops had disappeared, replaced with places Starbucks, Radio Shack and McDonald's. Now they even had a twenty-screen movie theatre where they pissed on your popcorn and called it "golden topping." Andy hated to think of how much money a man needed to take his family to a Bullies game. In the 1970s, he had spent endless hours running downtown Bayporte and even now could remember its streets and stores as vividly as scenes from a favorite movie. He could picture people entering and exiting Franklin's Department Store and Calvin's Shoes. Ditching school as rain pounded the city, he had daydreamed away entire afternoons at the Regency 6 Cinemas, buying a ticket and sneaking from one auditorium to the next until the more conscientious ushers ran him off. If you had one wish, Andy, would it be to go back thirty years and give life another try?

"That goddamn Joey," Andy said, tightening his grip around Annie's shoulders. "He follows me around like a bloody shadow. He's wearin me out. I told him today about how I used to own this town."

"Tell me again how you lost Bayporte. I'd love to hear it."

"I lost it in a poker game with some Chinks and

Pakis. I was drunk and they were cheatin. They cleaned me out."

They laughed, and he told her, "I talked to my kid at the cemetery today."

"Why did you do that?"

Andy shook his head. "Not sure. Just seemed like the right thing to do."

"You think about her a lot, hey?"

"Always have."

"You need to get over it. Life goes on," Annie said.

"I think," Andy told her, "that I'm gettin as weird as Joey. I stood there in that graveyard today and talked to my dead kid. No wonder Joey likes me so much. We have a lot in common."

"You're nothing like him. You've just had some hard times lately. We don't belong in skid row. We need to where we *do* belong."

"Yeah," Andy said. "Just as soon as we figure out where that is, we'll go there."

They walked on silence for a moment or two. Then, "Andy, don't drink anything more tonight. I need you sober. I can't rely on you when you're drunk."

"Don't rag on me."

"I'm not ragging." Her teeth were practically chattering from the cold. "I just need you to be mentally together."

"I *am* mentally together. The rest of the world is fucked."

Across the street, Marco Rigoni pointed at them. Andy recognized him as the man the railway cops had killed, but he had no idea why Rigoni was across the street pointing at him now. But then, looking over his shoulder, Andy saw Rockin Rod Brollar, the man who, years earlier, had died while trying to slash Andy's throat with a switchblade.

"All those years after my kid died," Andy said to Annie, hoping she hadn't noticed that two dead guys were following them, "my wife never told anyone the truth. Not the family, not the cops, no one. She told them it was SIDS or somethin. Can you imagine a woman like that, lyin to everyone to protect her man?"

"You have pretty strong feelings about your family."

"Well, they *are* my family. Or *were*."

"Then why not go see them? Tell them what's on your mind."

Andy shook his head. "Wouldn't accomplish nothin. Say, why didn't you stay at the mission tonight? Big Red invited ya."

She snarled. "I don't need their pity."

"But you go there every day. You eat their meals."

"I don't like Eccles. He doesn't like women," Annie told him.

"You don't like him and maybe he don't like you. There's no law sayin you gotta like each other."

Annie shivered. "It's so bloody cold, too! I can't remember ever being warm."

"Stop talkin about it and maybe you won't notice it so much." He paused. "You sang for me tonight. You sang for Kelly Wadham, too."

Annie sighed. "I sang while Flo died."

"It was for the best. Her time was up." He squeezed her shoulders. "You know somethin? You're the best thing that's happened to me in a long while."

She grunted. "Too bad for you."

He smiled. "You're a good sort, puttin up with me the way you do."

She smiled back. "Like the book says, *I'm OK, You're OK.*"

"Let's be OK together," Andy said, "and get our asses over to Dan's place before they turn out the lights and we fuckin freeze to death."

. . .

Dan and Bev lived in a handsome brick building just a few blocks from Pioneer Park. Their development, like those surrounding it, had been a mansion occupied by the robber barons of Bayporte. Over time, companies wanting to make quick, easy, big money had bought these mansions, chopped them up into units as small as five hundred feet and sold them as condominiums.

"Dammit!" Annie slapped at the rows of white buttons dotting the building's shiny black directory. "I can't remember which is theirs!:

"Don't worry." Andy had visited Dan and Bev enough times to observe a certain stubbornness in the door's closing mechanism. He had watched as the building's residents and their guests, distracted young people with cell phones pressed to their ears, went in and out, rarely troubling themselves to close the door securely.

Andy pulled the door and it swung open. *"Yeah! Get in and get warm, woman!"*

"Maybe," Annie said as she hurried into the heated lobby, "we should buzz Dan and tell him we're here."

"Maybe we'll just surprise him." Andy closed the door as he joined her inside.

"Ooh, so nice." Annie rubbed her arms, giggling.

They rode the elevator up to Dan's third-floor suite. "Smells good, eh?" Andy said as they sauntered down the hallway. "Reminds me when I played for the Bullies and we stayed in fancy places all the time."

"I hope they'll be happy to see us," Annie murmured as Andy knocked on Dan's door.

"Who's there?" Dan asked.

"It's us, Danny boy. We come to say hi."

They heard the deadbolt slide off. The door opened a crack. A sliver of face appeared. "How come you didn't buzz? Who let you in?"

"Front door was ajar when we got here," Andy

explained. "Didn't think we had to buzz just to say hi to an old friend."

"Fuckin security around here…" Dan muttered.

"Well, guy," Andy said, "we're here, and you're here, so's how about invitin us in for a splash of Canadian Comfort?"

After a long pause, during which Andy started to fear that he and Annie might actually be turned away, they saw the door close, then heard the chain slide off with a tiny rattle. They both let out big breaths as the door opened and they saw their friend Dan, his face looking not altogether pleased.

The two vagrants walked in. Celine Dion, from unseen speakers, wailed about an ended love affair. Andy and Annie looked around, all nods and smiles. A flat-screen TV dominated one wall; Oriental rugs lay strewn about on the dark hardwood floor. Abstract art covered a couple of walls. Dan's place featured high ceilings and recessed lighting. Andy nodded some more. Plenty of room to stretch your weary bones. Not too bad, Danny boy.

"I brought Annie."

"Long time, no see," she joked.

Bev, lying on a sofa against the wall, looked up at them without smiling. Above her hung a Jackson Pollock abstract print. She looks just like it, Andy thought with a smirk. She pulled at some of her lank dark hair and yawned. On the table next to her sat a bottle of Tia Maria and a liqueur glass.

"You wouldn't believe," Annie said to her, "how cold it is out there. We nearly froze to death walking over."

"Then you should have stayed home."

"We don't exactly *have* a home," Annie reminded her.

"Hard luck."

"So," Dan said, "what will it be? Canadian Comfort for two?"

"Coke for me, please," said Annie.

Dan nodded. "I'll get the drinks."

Andy and Annie sat on the sofa facing Bev. "So, Bev," Andy said, "how ya been keepin?"

"I feel the shits."

"That's too bad," said Annie, in a voice whose tone

suggested otherwise. "You didn't look so good last night, either."

Dan soon came back with their drinks. "Did Bev tell you that her divorce finally came through? It was a hassle, but at least now she's a free woman."

"I'll drink to that," said Andy, taking a sip of Canadian Comfort.

"My ex looks the same," said Bev. "*I'm* the one who's aged."

"Her kids showed up in court," said Dan. "I'm not sure why."

"It's because they're little shits," said Bev. "Always on their daddy's side."

"If I wasn't around anymore," Andy said, "I wonder how Annie would get along without me."

"Probably just fine," Annie replied. "You'd fall apart without me."

Andy smirked. "What a comfortin thought."

"No one," said Dan, "is leaving anyone anytime soon, I hope."

"Well," Annie said, "a woman must look after herself. She can't rely on a man for things."

Bev nodded. "Damn straight."

Annie sipped at her Coke. "A person should always do the right thing. You should be honest with yourself and others."

Andy threw back his head and hooted. "Are you kiddin? Who's honest? We're all liars, and fakers, suckin up and kissin ass to get what we want. And then we *don't* get we want because most of the time we don't *know* what we want. We want and want some more, and just keep discoverin that whatever we get is the wrong thing. It never ends."

"Thank you, professor," said Dan.

"Bev," said Andy, "can I ask you somethin?"

"No."

"Bev, at least let him *ask*," Dan said.

Bev sighed. "OK, ask."

"Well…" Andy faltered. He wanted to ask Bev to let Annie spend the night, because Dan would say no if Bev said no, but this was not the moment to ask.

"Bev," Andy asked, "do you think it will snow tonight?"

...

The Celine Dion CD ended, and the two couples sat in silence. Bev took some medicine and chased it down with a mouthful of Tia Maria, than lay back and let out a loud sigh.

Dan tsked. "Poor Bev, she's been all stressed out lately."

"Poor little lamb." Andy, a homeless alcoholic, wondered why he had just empathized with a spoiled divorcee whose biggest problems in life were boredom and menstruation.

"I'll tell you about hard living," Annie said. "I'm with Andy Kennedy. Every day is a challenge, and don't get me started on our *nights*."

"Oh? Am I as bad as all that?" Andy deadpanned. He drained his glass and poured himself some more Canadian Comfort. "I'm a bad influence on Annie. She was just a sweet young thing when I met her, innocent as could be, and I corrupted her."

"Andy," said Dan, "I used to think you were a winner, but now I'm not so sure. Why do you drink so much? Why can't you get your shit together?"

"Because," he said, "getting my shit together is a

smelly business."

"Always full of jokes, eh?" Dan asked.

"Annie's the problem," Andy said. "She's always raggin and naggin. I can't cope with her sometimes, so I drink. It stops the hurtin."

"I believe," Dan told him, "that you could become a handsome man again. If you could get off the booze and into rehab, you could have an American Express card, a fancy place to live, a car, all those things we all want."

Andy shrugged. "Been there, done that, Danny boy."

Dan leaned in closer. "But now all you have is the clothing on your back. Where did your fancy stuff go? Hey?"

Andy took another sip of Canadian Comfort. "If I had money, I would just spend it all on Annie. Get her whatever she wanted."

"All I want is you," said Annie.

"What *I* want and need," said Andy, "is to use the little boys' room."

"Use the one in the master bedroom." Dan pointed

to his right. "Bev has been stinking up the other one all day."

...

Andy, sitting on the toilet, wondered why Dan had made such a big deal about American Express cards and fancy cars. When he played for the Bullies, Andy had all that stuff and more. After flushing the toilet, he raised his arms to comb his hair and nearly fainted at the smell of his own body. Without asking permission to take a shower, he stripped naked and stepped into the stall. After standing under the hot water for a few refreshing minutes, he grabbed the bar of Ivory from the soapdish and worked up a generous lather. He had bathed so rarely that his hair, everywhere, was matted stiff, and he nearly wept with relief as he watched his filth disappear down the drain in an endless, inky stream. Finally, he massaged a handful of shampoo into his scalp, which finally stopped itching.

After drying off, he picked up his filthy, drenched underwear and stuffed it into his coat pocket. As Dan sat in the living room telling jokes, Andy, with a burglar's stealth, crept across his friend's bedroom, slid open the dresser's top drawer and plucked out a pair of Dan's Jockey briefs. Then, in a frenzy of silent activity, he snatched one of Dan's shirts, a pair of his slacks, one of his three parkas and, what the hell, a pair of shoes. His arms bulging with booty, Andy crept back into the washroom.

He switched on Dan's electric razor, slowly, and not altogether painlessly, shaved off his thick, stubborn growth of beard. Suddenly, Marco Rigoni and Rockin Rod Brollar appeared in the mirror's reflection. Both men sat on the toilet. Rigoni grinned at Andy's heap of putrid-smelling clothes on the washroom floor: a grown man's entire wardrobe. Rockin Rod just stared at Andy, as if he had never beheld such a fascinating, disturbing sight. Andy could remember, although he had tried hard to forget, much about that evening when he killed Rockin Rod under a bridge in Detroit.

Rockin Rod Brollar, Andy and a few other derelicts had gathered under that bridge around a bonfire, sharing a shoplifted bottle of Cisco Orange wine. Above them, tangles of Day-Glo graffiti swirled above them on the concrete bridge support. Rockin Rod, admiring the graffiti, said he was a connoisseur of street art and believed he knew the boys who had put it there. He told Andy and the others, for no reason that Andy could discern, that his sister had died during childhood and his brother had run off somewhere. Andy, who hated solitude as much as Rockin Rod did, guessed that his new acquaintance was all alone in the world. Tough and sneaky, attracted to danger and glory, Rockin Rod had applied to the Detroit Fire Department. After failing the firefighters' entrance examination, he took up boxing. His first opponent, a stringy black southpaw from the projects, seemed an easy enough. So Rockin Rod showed off for his friends, dancing, bobbing and weaving. He threw some good jabs and even got ahead in points until he inadvertently danced right into a left hook that knocked him cold. He woke up, eighteen hours later, in Detroit General Hospital, remembering how much he hated lefties.

Next, Rockin Rod found work bouncing rowdy drunks from local bars until his bosses caught him trying to pick the drunks' pockets. So, Rockin Rod Brollar, not knowing what else to do, did nothing at all. As a bum, he simply stole people's welfare checks or beat them up and shook them down. That evening, underneath the bridge, Rockin Rod Brollar and Andy Kennedy found that they had more in common than either man would have cared to admit. Rockin Rod, staring now at Andy in Dan's washroom, could recall nothing of his killer than big hands and feet.

Andy recalled holding court that evening underneath the bridge, talking mainly about hockey as they fed the sticks-and-trash bonfire as they passed around a bottle of Cisco. Laughing at his own cleverness—he would be the first to admit that he was a talker, not a listener—Andy spun mile-long yarns. He told these men about his boyhood in Bayporte, where hockey was a religion and he one of its finest choirboys. He'd been put on the ice and made to play against bigger boys; needing to be faster and smarter just to survive, he had learned his opponents' strengths and weaknesses. Andy Kennedy, he told these other men, had a Ph.D. in common sense from the School of Hard Knocks.

Staring into the bonfire and slurping syrupy wine, he told his cronies about the NHL. He dropped names, told them who jerked off to kiddie porn, who owed money to the Mob, who was shagging a teammate's wife. Andy's snickering rap, so shameless and unsparing in its salaciousness, made most of these men double over, hold their sides and beg him to stop.

But not Rockin Rod Brollar. Andy's colorful performance inspired in Rod an envy that bordered on rage. Why should this bullshit artist have enjoyed an adventurous life *and* the eloquence to thrill audiences with his tales? Where was the fairness when the Rockin Rods of the world had always struggled to communicate with other even in the simplest ways?

Well, Rockin Rod Brollar soon denied himself the opportunity to learn the art of the raconteur from one of its most polished practitioners, for the bonfire illuminated all of them vividly, and he spied Andy's sturdy shoes, which were vastly superior to his own rotting ones which scarcely protected his aching, blistered feet. Rockin Rod got up, pulled out his switchblade and said to Andy, in a livid boozy growl, 'I want them fuckin shoes.'

Rod saw Andy get up, too, and the man with the knife, muzzy from half a bottle of fortified wine, failed to understand how huge a blunder he had made in warning his victim of an imminent attack and his intention of stealing the other man's footwear. Andy, with Gatorade still in his muscles from years of hockey, had stayed mostly sober that evening and hardly resembled the wretch who now stood in Dan's washroom.

The bonfire had flickered like a strobe light as Rockin Rod lurched towards Andy, who immediately, and with some relief, observed that Rockin Rod had only a knife, not a gun, and a true wimp of a knife at that. Rockin Rod did not see the folly of making a drunken attack on a big, strong, mostly sober man. Rockin Rod needed to back off and apologize, but did not. He nearly fell into Andy's arms as he flailed about with his switchblade. Andy wrestled him into a police-style chokehold and soon Rockin Rod stopped moving. Andy, enraged by Rockin Rod's attack, let him fall unconscious to the ground, then picked him up by the armpit and pants leg and rammed him, head first, into the bridge's abutment. Rockin Rod Brollar's relatively brief but thoroughly violent existence ended with a sickening *crack!* Andy looked around and saw that the other men had run off. So he ran off, too, an act as natural for him as breathing. He hustled away from Rockin Rod Brollar and that bridge abutment with the same urgency as when he had felt when chasing the puck around the rink. He bolted, really, as if being pursued by his usual enemies—women, children, parents, bosses, institutions, traditions, commitments, obligations, conventions. He ran as if trying to fly, to become airborne and leave his own awful body.

After hanging up Dan's bath towel, Andy shrugged and smiled at Rockin Rod, as if saying, No hard feelins, hey? Rod, smiling back, grabbed his own throat and rolled his eyes comically. Observing how content, even happy, Rockin Rod seemed in death, Andy for a moment wished that their duel had ended differently. But he *had* won, that night in Detroit and in all subsequent battles.

"Andy!" called Annie. "What are you doing in there?"

"Droppin a deuce," he called back. Looking at Rockin Rod Brollar and Marco Rigoni, he thought, *I'm alive and you're dead, but who's really better off?*

Marco Rigoni put his hands together and offered Andy a small but compassionate prayer that this homeless man would survive this brutally cold night. Andy, never a Christian and often an atheist, nodded thanks for the prayer and forgot about it.

"Hey Danny boy." Andy emerged and stood before everyone in the living room. "How's about another splash of Canadian Comfort?"

Annie stared at her man, mouth wide open. "Andy! What happened to you?"

"And how come you're wearing Dan's clothes?" Bev asked.

Dan shook his head. "I don't mind a bit. You need that clothing much more than I do. You sure look sharp."

"I felt like I needed to get cleaned up a bit," Andy

said.

"You sure are a handsome man," said Annie. "When you're all cleaned up."

Andy laughed. "I'm a handsome man even when I'm filthy dirty." He added, "It's sure nice to be somewhere warm. I've known lots of guys who froze to death, either here in Canada or down in the northern States durin the winter. They died of frostbite or somethin. I would wake up somewhere in the frost and snow, and look around and see guys layin there, blue and dead. Then I'd say hi to the ones that survived, and we'd all get up and go about the business of another day of meaningless existin."

Dan shook his head. "I can't relate to any of that. I've never lived that way. I've always tried to make myself as comfortable as possible."

"There was this one guy," Andy went on. "He froze to death in Chicago. His buddy didn't want to freeze, but all the shelters were full, so he went to the hospital. The nurse said, 'You can't stay here because this is a hospital, not a shelter. You'll have to spend the night outside, but keep walking, because if you don't keep moving, you'll die of hypothermia.' So the guy went outside, lay down and said, 'Jack Frost? Here I am. Come and get me.' And he did."

"I've heard," Dan said, "that freezing to death is the most painless way to go. The mental patients get released, they become homeless and the authorities probably hope those poor buggers will freeze to death so they won't be a blight on the community any longer. I think that when we die, we go to the same place as Hitler and Pol Pot, and that's nowhere. No-fucking-where. I'm sure of it."

"So," replied Andy, "if nothin happens to us after we die, we have nothin to worry about. Then why the hell does everyone get bent out of shape worryin about it?"

"Because we don't fucking know," said Annie.

"I'm going wherever Danny's going," said Bev. "Who would want to live forever, anyway? A person would get bored."

Andy grinned. That goddamn Bev was no candidate for heaven, if such a place existed. He knew she'd been a hooker who'd gone straight for a while, even gotten married and had kids. Out of restlessness, she had gone back into the illicit life for a time. Now she's with Dan, pretendin she's Mary bloody Poppins. Lookin a bit long in the tooth now, but nothin a facelift and boob job couldn't fix. She could probably suck the chrome off a trailer hitch. Not bad, not bad at all. He wouldn't kick her out of bed.

"Why don't you take a picture?" Bev asked as Andy stared at her for several long moments. "In my day, I was pretty hot stuff."

"Not so bad now," replied Andy.

"Don't flirt," admonished Annie.

"Men," said Dan, "have always admired Bev. But she's mine now. Once she gets to feeling better, we'll go out and start spending money again."

"But for now, I'm just a sick lady who needs her rest. I'm getting ready for bed. It was nice seeing you again. Make sure the lobby door closes properly on your way out and think warm thoughts so you don't die of hypothermia like your friends did."

"Nice place you got here." Andy looked around and smiled.

"Maybe that's why you come here so often," Bev said.

Andy shook his head. "Not that often."

"Annie stayed here last night. Sometimes you've been here for close to a week."

"Not me. Not us." Andy frowned. "You have us confused with someone else."

"I don't think so." Bev took a sip of Tia Maria. "We don't have too many homeless people flopping here."

"I spent last night here," Annie conceded. "But that was the first time in quite a while."

"You've spent many more nights here than you know."

"You're a lying bitch," said Annie.

Bev sat up. "And you're a stupid old hag. Don't come into *my* home and call *me* a lying bitch. It's very rude, and you are the last person in this world who should be calling other people names."

"Shit!" Andy glowered at Annie. "What's your problem? You're supposed to be an educated woman who knows about good manners and all that."

Annie glowered back at him. "I *am* an educated woman and I *know* about good manners. But I also have pride, like everyone else."

"My idea," said Dan, "was for Andy to stay with us till he could get his life back together. I didn't want anything in return, just the satisfaction of seeing a good man get himself straightened away."

"You're very kind, Dan," said Annie.

Dan shook his head. "But that offer is no longer valid."

"Gee, that's too bad." Andy knocked back another shot of Canadian Comfort.

"You're such a fool." Annie let out a derisive little chuckle that sounded like a hiccup. "You're always drunk and vulgar. You've thrown away every opportunity you've ever had. With you it's just drink, drink, drink. You're hopeless."

"Havin to took after you all the goddamn time drives me to drink, drink, drink." He paused. "Maybe, if I tried really hard, I could give up the booze."

"Do you think," Annie said to Dan, "we could stay the night here?"

"You will have to make other arrangements."

"We should be leavin now," Andy said.

"It's for the best," Dan said.

"They've made up their minds," Annie told Andy. "Let's go."

"Shut up and stop bein such a pain in the ass!" Andy swayed as he stood, and as he tried to sit, his butt nearly missed the seat. "You wanna spend the night in Pioneer Park, cuddlin me for warmth? Dan and Bev are kickin us out, so we're goin to Pioneer Park!"

Annie crossed her legs and folded her arms. "I have never spent a night in Pioneer Park."

"Oh sure you have," said Bev.

"Annie's lyin," Andy said. "We've spent nights out there, and in worse places, too. Good thing Pioneer Park is so big. There's plenty of room for all of us down-and-outers."

"You must have me confused," said Annie, "with some woman desperate enough to spend the night in the park."

"You've also spent a few nights sleepin in Boylan's

smelly old tent near the mission," Andy reminded her.

"Never again." Annie shuddered. "Never again. I have people I can call, people who care about me and want to help."

"Then call them," said Bev. "You can use my cell phone."

"My brother," Annie went on, "is an engineer with a great job. I come from a family of achievers. I would hate for them to see me like this."

"To hell with that nonsense," Dan told her. "If you have family out there who will take you in and help you get off the street, go to them. Same to you, Andy."

"But," Annie said, "if I went back to my people, it would be the end of my relationship with Andy. I need him as much as he needs me. We'll work it out together. He'll marry me if I want him to. Right?"

He winked at her. "Right, sweetie."

She brightened a bit. "See? We get along great when he's not drunk and crazy."

"I'm about to fall asleep." Bev closed her eyes. "Goodnight."

"One last thing." Andy turned to Dan. "How's

about givin us somethin to eat? Somethin to go."

Bev opened her eyes. "Denny's is open all night."

"Got no money for Denny's."

"The man," said Dan, "just asked for something to eat. Am I gonna give him something? Damn straight I am." He looked at Andy. "You know what I got for you? I got half a goddamn sub sandwich that I was gonna save as a bedtime snack. You need it more than I do. It's got cold cuts, mustard, mayo and onions. You like that?"

Andy licked his lips. "Sounds yummy."

"So that's what I'm gonna do. I'm gonna give you that damn sandwich that's in the fridge. I'm not too proud to give a sandwich to a hungry man." He ducked into the kitchen and came back seconds later with a sandwich wrapped in pattered white paper. He handed it to Andy, who slipped it into the pocket of the parka Dan had given him.

"Enjoy," said Dan.

"I thank you muchly," said Andy. "See ya, Bev." He helped Annie out of her chair and the two headed for the door.

"Goodbye and good luck," Bev replied.

Back in the hallway, Annie said, "What are we going to do now? I'm about ready to curl up and fall asleep right now."

"Yeah, and the first person in this building who found you would call the cops, and they would put you back on the street.

"Maybe," Annie said, "I would get lucky and die before the cops got here."

"Forget that," Andy muttered. "Your luck don't run that good."

They rode the elevator back down and Andy held open the lobby's front door. Annie stood in the doorway and shivered. "Too cold. We'll both die. Andy, let's just huddle in the lobby and take our chances with the cops."

"No can do, babe." He gave her a gentle push out the door and followed her. They both heard the click of the door and Andy grimaced, wondering if Annie had the right idea, hiding out in the lobby for the night. Well, too late now.

Out of habit, they walked towards skid row, away

from Pioneer Park; Andy suppressed a momentary desire to take off, just run away and leave Annie forever and try to forget her had ever met her.

They walked on in silence until they reached Grand Street. The Bank of Toronto's old-fashioned tower clock said one-fifty. Above them, the moon remained huge and indifferent.

Annie said, with gritted teeth, "I wouldn't have stayed with those people if they had paid me."

"Why not?"

"That bitch Beverly! I can remember when she was getting pissed each night and putting out for every horny guy in town."

"Dan thinks you're rude to Bev." He smirked at how their brisk walk had energized Annie. "Let's stop for a minute and have a bite of sandwich. I've got a Hershey bar for dessert."

"Eat it yourself. I don't like cold cuts."

"Have some anyway. You don't get enough to eat. That's why you're sick all the time." His breathing grew harder. "You're fuckin impossible. No wonder Dan asked us to leave. You heard him in there. He wanted me to stay with them and dry out. He wants me to become a superstar again."

"Then why won't you accept his help?"

"Because," Andy told her, "bein a superstar is hard work."

Annie burst out laughing. Andy grabbed her by the lapels and shook her. "Don't you ever fuckin laugh at me again! I'll knock you on your ass!" He snarled, and his breath came out in a long stream of vapor that went up her nose. "I'd be doin you a favor if I hit you. I might knock some sense into you."

She glared at him for several moments, and he backed off a bit.

"This sandwich"—he held it under her nose as if it were a bottle of ice water and they were stranded in the Mojave Desert—"is all. We got. Till mornin." He took a couple of long, laborious breaths. "Eat some."

"*You* eat it."

"Watch me." Sneering, he unwrapped it, took a big bite and chewed for what seemed forever. After swallowing several times, he licked his lips and said, "Like I told you. Gotta get you. Settled in. For the night."

"Maybe we should call my brother and ask him to come get me."

"What's his. Number?" Andy asked, swallowing a bite of submarine sandwich and still breathing hard.

"I don't know."

Andy chuckled. "What's his. Address?"

She shrugged.

"Well. That'll make it. A bit harder. Findin him."

"He's my brother, Andy. I'm always welcome in his home."

"Probably. Don't know. You're alive." He finished the sandwich and said, after waiting a few minutes to catch his breath, "You had the right idea to sleep in Dan's lobby and hope the cops didn't come by."

"Well, we didn't. You know, we were having such a good day until you started drinking. 'Oh, let's go see Kelly Wadham and have a Coke.' Yeah, right. You're an alcoholic. There's no such thing as you going into a bar and only having a Coke."

Andy sighed. "We can talk about my personal flaws later. Right now, we need to find you a place to sleep."

Annie rolled her eyes. "Who cares? I get a place to sleep, I wake up later and what do I have to look forward to? Another day of wandering around and another night of worrying about where I'm going to sleep."

"Well, you need a place to sleep, and we're runnin out of options, old thang."

. . .

"Home sweet home," Andy muttered as, half an hour later, he bent down to unzip the tent's entrance.

"I don't like this," Annie muttered.

"Me neither. But it's this or dealin with Jack Frost."

Annie shook her head.

"Just for tonight, babe. Tomorrow we'll find somethin better. I promise." He clasped her hands in his. "Get in there and get warm. You'll fall asleep fast and feel much better in the mornin. We'll go to the mission, have some breakfast and make some plans."

"What about you?"

Andy shrugged. "Oh, I'll find somewhere. I always do." He reached inside the tent and gave its occupant a firm shake. "Hey, sleepin beauty! Wake up!"

"Who dat?"

"It's your fairy godmother. Wake up, guy. I brought my old lady. She's cold and needs to get warm. Be nice to her, and tomorrow I'll buy you a bottle of Canadian Comfort."

"Hey—?"

"Move over, Boylan. Annie's comin in. It's bloody freezin out here."

With some assistance from Andy, Boylan rolled over and made room for Annie. Andy watched her ease herself in and as soon as she lay by Boylan's side, he blew her a kiss, zipped up the tent and took a few minutes to stand up straight.

Stupefied by exhaustion but relieved at having gotten Annie tucked in, Andy traipsed towards the nearest bus stop, hoping that at least one more would be going his way until transit service ended for the night. He thought back to the 1970s, when the buses stopped running at midnight. People complained, but Andy felt they shouldn't have, because Bayporte wasn't on the map yet and there was nothin to do and nowhere to go at night.

He sat on a crumbling bench for half an hour. When the bus arrived, he stuck one of Vince de George's bus tickets into the validator, nodded at the driver and collapsed into one of the seats. He looked outside and saw the Penis Theatre, one of his favorite porn hangouts, where he had snored away whole hours while the men surrounding him smoked crack or did other things.

As the bus lumbered past the TransCanada Railway Station, Andy thought back to all the times he had stolen rides to the rest of Canada to escape some sort of trouble at home, and then returned to Bayporte as a stowaway in those same cars. Sometimes he liked to think of himself as a disabled war veteran, shell shocked in Vietnam, Iraq or Afghanistan, shipped home bitter and homeless. Never thought I would end up here for good, or that my life would get so bad. He thought of Annie, now safe and warm for a few hours in Boylan's funky old tent. Like she said: Survivin tonight, but what about tomorrow?

He rode the bus all the way back to Southlands cemetery, where he had shoveled dirt that day. Soon he found Li Wong's mausoleum, fingering the padlock. Nice and rusted. It'll come off easy enough. Backing up a few steps, he kicked at it as hard as he could, then kicked at it some more, making a racket that he was sure would wake someone, somewhere. The lock shattered and fell to the ground. "Move over, Li, you've got company."

...

Andy stretched out on Li Wong's marble floor, oddly comforted by the sound of the howling wind outside and the dark sky that showed no signs at all of getting lighter. Tonight would be easy; no cops or punks would be roaming around in a cemetery, looking to victimize the Andys of the city. Nobody would think that a homeless guy would break into a mausoleum just to squat for a night.

At first, he felt too tired to sleep. He fantasized about springtime evenings and perfumed ladies in white dresses. Then he stared out into the darkness and thought about his father, who had been killed on Fairview Avenue and buried in Southlands. A good egg, his old man, and good eggs always flew straight up to heaven, if you believed what the preacher said. Mum? Neither good enough for heaven nor bad enough for hell. Where would she go? And what about Andy, with his sinning, drinking old soul? Or Annie…?

He had to outlive her. She couldn't survive without him at her side, no matter what she thought. He'd listened as she carried on about Julliard, her rich daddy, her family's refined tastes and delicate sensibilities, her engineer brother whose door remained forever open to her.

Yeah, right.

Annie had learned very little about street survival and seemed to take forever to learn each minor skill. A slow learner, that one, or maybe she just had a poor mentor. Perhaps, as she had often said, she would die first and stop being his problem. Annie would rather have frozen to death than crawl in with Boylan, but there she was, asleep with the rest of the city. That woman, Andy thought with a smile, sure has a gift for snoozin. In exchange for her tent privileges, of course, she would have to get friendly with Boylan, not that he could do much at his age and state of decay. Andy felt lucky that Boylan hadn't put up any kind of fuss when Andy deposited Annie into his tent, and he thought: I should try to remember to buy him a bottle of Canadian Comfort like I promised.

He thought of other things, better things. He felt grateful to be hidden away from all potential predators, and soon he became drowsy and peaceful. Sleepin in a mausoleum, he told himself, isn't so bad if you don't mind who your roomies are.

"Say goodnight, Li," Andy murmured as he drifted off into a deep, long slumber.

IV

Andy, after sleeping surprisingly well in the boneyard, arrived on time at Pawlowski's home in east Bayporte. The house, old and big, had been built during the postwar boom, when bigger was better. This one had faded, peeling paint and a spacious backyard filled with every kid of hunk. Andy stood there and looked around at the heaps of soiled computers, three-legged desks, car parts and TV sets.

He watched a heavy-shouldered old man made his way down the back stairs. A big old man in a big old house on the "affordable" side of Bayporte, where even being a bum was expensive. Pawlowski's old spread, as ugly as it was, had to be worth a million bucks or more, Andy guessed.

"How's it goin, eh?" Andy said with a wave and smile. "Are you Mr. Pawlowski?"

The old man nodded. "Somethin you want?"

"Reverend sent me by. He said you wanted some help around here."

Pawlowski squinted. "Got a name?"

"Kennedy. Andy Kennedy."

"I know that name from somewhere. You used to be somebody?"

Andy shrugged. "Used to be. I played for the Bullies."

"Yeah, I watch hockey. Bullies almost won Stanley Cup once or twice."

Andy nodded. "Once or twice. Maybe one of these days they'll do it."

"So now you're here. I need strong man to help me. You that man?"

"I played hockey for a livin."

"You life heavy objects?" Pawlowski asked.

"Show me the object."

"Lift car engine?"

Andy laughed. "Fuck no!"

"Me neither." He pointed at a TV set. "Lift that up."

Andy went over to the TV, which wasn't huge but

wasn't small, either. He kept his back straight and lifted with his legs. Grunting and straining, he hoisted the appliance. "Fuckin heavy," he said, his face red.

"Put it down," said Pawlowski. "Step aside." He went over and picked up the TV as if it were made of Styrofoam, then transferred it from arm to arm and set it back down.

"You're a strong man," Andy told him. "You own this whole place?"

Pawlowski nodded. "Own it all. Sold the others."

"Worth a few bucks, eh?"

"Worth plenty. Had offers to sell, turned them down. Lots of money in bank, too. Set for ten lifetimes."

Andy pointed to the computers in the corner of the yard. "Those things work?"

"Some work, some not."

"Why you collectin dead computers?" Andy asked. "Just a bunch of crap."

Pawlowski shook his head. "No crap here. Everythin has value. Dead computers made of plastic, glass, metal. Worth plenty."

"How come," Andy asked, rubbing his chin, "if some of these computers still work, people gave them to you?"

"People stupid," said Pawlowski. "People spoiled brats. Their friend gets a new computer, they need a new one, too. Computer they got ain't good enough now, so they want to get rid of it and I take it. Fine with me." Then, "You come here to talk or work?"

"How much you payin?" Andy asked.

"Fifty dollar for eight-hour workday."

"Not much money for a grown man."

"Oh? You got a mortgage to pay off?"

"No," Andy told him, "but I'm still a grown man with livin expenses."

"Take it or leave it,' Pawlowski said.

"OK, boss," Andy replied.

"Get in the truck." Pawlowski pointed to a soiled gray Ford. Within a few minutes of riding around with Pawlowski, Andy decided he would have been better off just telling the old man to go fuck himself. Pawlowski's truck desperately needed new shock absorbers, and the two men bounced around so hard that Andy feared he might end up in Pawlowski's lap. The truck went up one street and down the next on this clear, cool morning. Andy always enjoyed watching the city wake up on a sunny day. He smiled at the pretty young women all dressed up for a day of office work; years earlier, they had smiled at him, too. Travel always made him smile, even if it was just driving around with a crabby old fart like Pawlowski. Andy had enjoyed riding the trains for days at a time, never buying a ticket and always jumping off once his booze ran out and he had to look for day labor. Even then, the work made him feel temporarily rejuvenated and optimistic. He fastened his seat belt in Pawlowski's truck and worried about Annie. Where was she? He couldn't stop worrying until he saw her for himself and knew she was alive and breathing. She probably likes this, he thought. She likes knowin that I worry about her all the time. Well, Annie, I hope you're happy, because you're breakin my balls.

"So," Pawlowski asked, how did you like it?"

"Hey?"

"You know. The hockey life. The pussy."

Andy shrugged. "That happened a long time ago. Haven't thought about it much lately."

"They say you street people bumhole each other for drug money. Is that so?"

"Maybe some, but not me. Never bought or sold it. Anyway, I'm gettin too old for that."

Pawlowski shook his head. "Never too old for some things. How old are you?"

"Fifty-five."

"I'm nearly seventy. Like my lovin as much as ever. Don't need hard-on pills, either. Get it on with the old lady every other night, and this job presents many opportunities to meet lovely ladies who are interested in making new friends."

"Kinda doubt that," Andy muttered.

"Do you? It's very simple: You enter their home to collect their donations, and pretty soon you're entering other things."

"Good way to get herpes and AIDS," Andy said.

"No. Always wear a condom, then no problem. Always do it with a woman who hasn't done every man in town. The women I screw don't have diseases.

All they got is gratitude."

"Don't they mind your filthy clothes? Don't you get their nice clean beds all dirty?"

"Don't do it in bed. Do it standing up, in the basement, in the kitchen. Who cares where? We'll see one of these ladies this morning." Pawlowski gave Andy a sly smile. Andy didn't know that Pawlowski knew how to smile.

"When we get there," Andy said, "you go have your fun and I'll wait here in the trunk."

"Good plan." They drove along Commerce Street, stopping a few times to go into houses and come back out with huge green garbage bags filled to bursting with secondhand clothing. Andy liked it about as much as he enjoyed digging graves.

"My favorite." Pawlowski pointed to a house with a stucco exterior. Nice woman in there. Very nice."

Andy nodded. "I hear ya. Take your time and give her one for me. I'm pretty sure I'll be here when you get back."

"You can stand at the window and watch. Free adult entertainment, no subscription required."

Pawlowski took off to see his lady friend, and Andy sat and stared at nothing for several long minutes. While this section of town had never really been his turf, he recalled having come out here sometimes with his friends in his teens, cruising for girls and looking for trouble to get into. One night, they happened upon a fornicating couple in a locked car. Andy wanted to rock the car back and forth, maybe even roll it over onto its side, but his friends lost interest and walked away, so he did too. But the experience of watching those two grinding bodies, whose audible grunts and moans of pleasure turned him on back then, stayed with him even now, and he squirmed in Pawlowski's truck, aroused. Did he want a woman now? No. Maybe. Annie? No, not her, not that way. What he wanted, he supposed, was to be a kid again, young and optimistic, roaming about with his pals and generally being a badass.

Andy got out of the truck and went over to the side entrance of the house, the one Pawlowski had used. Inside, the old man was hard at work with the woman.

"Hell yeah," Pawlowski said.

"Put your cock in me!" the woman cried out. "I'm gonna come on your cock. Fuck me till I come."

"Hell yeah," said Pawlowski. "Hell yeah."

The woman, nearly as old as Pawlowski, saw Andy and waved for him to come in. Andy shook his head and returned to the truck.

Over the years, he had seen and done most of what street life offered sexually: Homeless people having intercourse in public, men doing women by the dozens, men doing each other. He pictured the women with whom he had done things: standing up, sitting down, spread eagled, underneath, on top. Women needing and pleading, yearning and burning. Annie. They had met in a downtown bar, and when they discovered they had been born in the same hospital, their friendship began. He kissed her; she slipped him the tongue. He felt her up; she already seemed old and lumpy.

But they could confide in each other. They were both alone and lonely. Andy said he was freaked out by the AIDS crisis and didn't know if he wanted to become sexually active. Plus, he told her, he couldn't get it up because of his boozing. Still, they got a cheap room and ravished each other for an entire weekend until they lay side by side, sweaty and exhausted. Love, you turn me inside out. Love, you are a force I cannot resist; I will do as you wish. Love, I am your slave.

Pawlowski returned to the truck, drove this way and that, and soon they were on Fairview Avenue, heading towards the cemetery. Shit, Andy thought, I shoveled dirt there yesterday. I can't seem to get away from that place. For reasons he could not comprehend, he began visualizing his parents on their wedding night, or perhaps just after their honeymoon, emerging from their rented luxury car and bounding up the steps of their Fairview Avenue house. His father looked young in these images; of course, he had been a handsome man in his youth, and a sedan in the heavy rain had saved him from the necessity of growing old and the possibility of getting ugly. Andy's mother, radiant and girlish with her new husband, but even then, somehow, an angry young woman. Far more prone to violence, she, when displeased with Andy, would shake her little boy by the shoulders and then slap him till his ears rang.

"Let's wait her a minute," Andy said to Pawlowski.

"How come?"

"Because I said so."

Pawlowski shook his head. "Strange bum."

The newly married Mr. and Mrs. Kennedy moved into their house in 1958 and stayed there for the rest of their lives. Andy watched his own conception and birth, nine months speeded up into a few minutes, and felt ashamed of himself for thinking of such things. "Southlands Cemetery," he said aloud.

"What about it?" asked Pawlowski.

"My people are buried there."

"Nice for them."

"And I worked there yesterday," Andy told them. "I slept there last night."

Pawlowski frowned. "Slept in graveyard? Where, under trees?"

"No, in a muasoleum."

"Thought mausoleums were locked."

Andy nodded. "It was, but I broke in."

Pawlowski shook his head again. "I got bum

working for me who breaks into mausoleum so he can sleep."

They reached their destination, a house half a block from the one Andy grew up in. "You go in alone," he said to Pawlowski. "I probably know these people. I sort of grew up around."

"So go in with me and say hi."

Andy shook his head. "No way. They haven't seen me in ages. They don't know I've gone downhill."

"Middle-aged bum, sleeping in mausoleum, worries about what the neighbors will think." Pawlowski clambered out of the truck. Andy sat back, closed his eyes and imagined his mother with her pruning shears, cutting away the parts of the neighbors' big maple tree that dangled onto the Kennedys' property. Andy called it the Saddys' Tree, although they lived next door for a relatively brief time. Andy's mother attacked the Saddys' Tree until her death. He remembered being outside when Rikia Saddy emerged from her house naked.

"Miz Saddy…!"

She smiled. "Hello, Andy! Nice day out, hey? I'd

love to chat for a bit, but I have places to go."

"But you're naked!"

She frowned, looked down and stood paralyzed. He hurried over and walked her back to her house.

"Can't have you doin this," he murmured. "You'd get into nothin but trouble." He settled her on her sofa and put a blanket around her.

She quickly regained her composure. "Why cover me up? I'm not embarrassed about being naked in front of you."

"But I am. Don't do that again, OK? They don't like naked ladies walkin around here. You might catch cold or they would call the cops."

Rikia nodded and relaxed. "Thank you for your help. It's nice that we have this chance to visit. Sometimes people live next door to each other for ages and don't trouble themselves to become acquainted."

Andy nodded, wondering why this particular neighbor thought it was OK to get acquainted with him in this manner. "Is your husband home? Maybe he should know about this."

She shook her head. "He's in Toronto on business. And no, he doesn't need to know about this. I think I should put something on."

"Good idea."

...

Weeks later, Rikia hired Andy to mow her lawn. Under the bright sun, he worked so hard that his muscles burned and he sweated like a slave.

"I'm making iced tea," Rikia called out. "Want some?"

Andy turned around and smiled at the sight of her in a yellow summer dress and a wide-brimmed hat. He swore she was the sexiest thing he had ever seen. Although he didn't especially like iced tea, he joined her on the terrace for a glass.

"Cigarette?" she asked.

"No thanks."

"Don't smoke, eh? Good for you."

He shook his head. "No, ma'am. I couldn't do much on the hockey rink if I smoked."

She nodded. "Cigarettes are poisonous. I've tried to quit a few times but it was just too hard."

"I drink sometimes," he confided.

She smiled. "Well, a person has to have a vice." Then, "I want to talk to you about the day you saw me come out of the house naked."

He shrugged.

"Andy, do you know anything about mental illness?"

"It doesn't sound like much fun."

"You're right, it's not. Well, that morning, I was having some trouble with mental illness. That's why I went outside naked. Have you told anyone about it?"

"No, ma'am. It's nobody's business."

Rikia smiled. "Good. Then it'll just be our little secret."

"Fine with me, ma'am."

"One more thing, Andy. My name isn't ma'am, it's Rikia. Call me that."

"OK, Rikia."

"Andy." She rolled around his name in her mouth, as if tasting it. "OK if I call you Andrew?"

"If you want to," he said.

"Andy Kennedy."

"Rikia Saddy," he said.

She extended her hand. "A pleasure to meet you, Andrew."

He shook it. "Same here, Rikia."

...

Sitting in Pawlowski truck, Andy thought of that big yellow house Rikia and her husband had lived in. He remembered her as the first woman who had ever captivated his soul. The others had been mere girls, simple and selfish; Rikia had brought style, sophistication and class to Fairview Avenue.

Her husband, a man whose important work involved flights to Toronto and New York City, seemed gone as often as not. Theirs was the biggest house on the block, and Andy supposed that the trick to getting a woman like Rikia was to make enough money to offer her things like a big house and beautiful clothes.

"Andrew," she had asked him, "do you like school?"

"Not much."

"Do you know many pretty girls there?"

"One or two, maybe."

Rikia smirked. "I'm sure you know all the pretty girls at school. Aren't you in love with any of them?"

He squirmed a bit. "Don't have much time for fallin in love. Right now my life is passin tests and playin hockey."

"Are you in love with me?" she asked.

"Hey?"

"Don't I obsess you?"

"I don't know what that means."

"It means," she explained, "that you think about a person all the time. Is that how you feel about me?"

Andy said nothing but his face turned red.

"Obsession," she continued, "is not necessarily a bad thing. Hockey is one of your obsessions, and I'm sure you're a fine player."

He nodded. "I'm countin on playin for the Bullies one day soon. My coaches tell me I'm good enough."

"I have talents, too," Rikia said. "I'm hoping we'll get to know each other well enough for you to discover what my talents are."

He swallowed hard.

Rikia went to watch Andy at hockey practice. She hugged herself in the chilled air and kept looking around, as if unable to tell him apart from the others; after watching him—or was it someone else?—score a few goals, she left. She insisted that he come over for lunch one day so they could sit and visit at length. "Our time," she called it.

"I'm not like you, Rikia," he told her, sounding envious rather than angry. "I don't live in a big house and I don't know anythin about wine. I don't have any fancy talk."

"Your talk is fine," she said. "Do you still think about me when we're not together?"

"Always."

"Tell me about your fantasies," Rikia said.

He gave her a small, nervous laugh. "Oh, I couldn't do that."

She giggled and said, "Tell me."

"Well"—he cleared his throat—"it's just that there's this bully pickin on you, and I come along. I straighten him out."

Rikia smiled. "You are a chivalrous young man.

Does your mother know about our visits?"

He shook his head. "None of her bloody business."

"I agree. I like your attitude. Your mother doesn't approve of me, does she?"

"My mother," Andy said, "doesn't approve of anyone or anythin."

Another time, she asked him, "Do you believe in God?"

"No, not the way most people do, like goin to church and readin the Bible."

"God is love," she told him. "He's not to be found just in church. He exists wherever love is. There are no miracles or accidents in this world. We are totally insignificant and our lives are beyond our control. It's when we forget this that we get into trouble."

Rikia died in the 1985 fire that destroyed part of her big yellow house. Andy, on a Bullies road trip in New York City or Boston, called home and his mother told him that the Saddys' house was on fire and she hoped that the fire would kill that miserable maple tree that had given her so much grief.

Andy wanted to fly home for Rikia's funeral but

decided against it. He also considered putting flowers on her grave in Southlands, if she was buried there, but didn't do that, either. Still, he thought about her—he still avoided the word *obsessed* because that's what the reporters called stalkers and other creeps—and remembered what she'd said about how all things were simply meant to be.

V

Annie sang to herself as the stared out her room's grimy window. She wore her rayon turquoise robe, pilfered from Save on Clothes; she'd plucked it off the rack, stuffed it into her coat and walked out as the security guard busied himself on his cell phone. In her room, she collapsed into an old, much-abused easy chair and stared for the longest time at a print of what appeared to be a black jazzman playing a saxophone.

Bebopbebop

Doooodooooodoooo

Bebopbebop

When she was around music, her world became a better place. What an elixir she had! Melodies floated about in her head like butterflies, transporting her to a better place and time, when a stellar musical career appeared to be her destiny. Her father, too, wanted so much for his Annie to distinguish herself—and thus her family—through music. First she would attend

Julliard, then fly overseas and study at one of the eminent European conservatories, if she was really as gifted as everyone claimed. Her star would never descend, just as her grandmother's had never risen. Go out there, the old woman had told her, and dazzle the universe. Always remember what it means to me, and make it your life's goal.

And a month later, Annie's grandmother died.

Annie's first tragedy.

Her second one happened when she was still so new to Julliard that she had trouble finding the ladies' room. She received a summons to the dean's office and found her mother waiting there with this news: Your father is ill. We must return to Bayporte immediately.

On the flight home, over the Prairies, her mother became more specific. Your father, she said, is dead. In the taxi ride to their front door, she added: He jumped off the Tyson River Bridge.

Annie, too shocked to say anything, remained virtually mute for days. Her mother sat down in private with her and said: We need to talk about some things. You can't go back to Julliard because there's no money for that. Your musical education is over.

Why? Annie asked, although she really didn't want an answer.

Your father invested most of his money in an overseas gold mind that yielded nothing. We're not quite broke. We have enough for your brother to finish his doctorate in engineering. Money is nice, but engineering is *important.*

So Annie sat in that big ugly chair in the Pattison Hotel as hours crept by. She could not have said how long she remained in that chair, nor did she especially care. Kind old Stelfox knocked on her door and asked, *Annie, are you OK in there? Is there anything you need? A Coke from the machine downstairs?*

Oh, no thanks, arthritic old man. I'm probably less needy than you are. No Coke for me; I'm already sweet enough. But thank you for reminding me that I'm still alive. I keep forgetting.

Her day had started with music. She crawled out of Boylan's tent, humming Kelly Wadham songs as Boylan snored. She could not have said when exactly she awoke, and those hours of sleep hadn't rejuvenated her as much as Andy had said they would. Once out of that tent. Annie told herself that Boylan had probably saved her life and she would try hard to forgive him for that. After stretching and yawning, she headed out of the alleyway. The sun was climbing the horizon but a few stars remained visible.

Leave me alone, she had told Boylan, knowing that she had no right to say such a thing and he had no intention of doing as she said. So she relaxed and let him feel her up, and she even ground her bottom into his groin when he seemed unable to get an erection. After a little while, they both lost interest and fell asleep.

Walking alone now, she yawned some more. Always sleepy, and she guessed that beat never sleepy. Through sleep, she became able to escape the squalor and despair and lose herself in exciting dreams. She smoothed out her robe and puttered along, looking up at the fading stars and thinking: Which star is which? And can they see me down here in skid row? I wish I could go up there and be with them.

She stopped in the nearest church, groped her way to an aisle seat and saw an angel who said, "There is but one God, the only God, the creator of the universe!"

Annie thought: I'm a good Catholic, been one all my life, so how come He lets me sleep in bums' tents?

She would have preferred a bigger, fancier church, but this morning her body felt so leaden that she decided any place of worship would do. By now, churches were beginning to seem the same to her, anyway. The Natives came here to pray for deliverance from the white man's tyranny. Annie's mum had always feared these red-skinned people, with their alcoholism, bad breath and standoffs with the Canadian National Police. Don't make friends with them, Mum had said, and don't lend them any money.

As the organist began playing, Annie closed her eyes and let the music wash over her, then she opened them and looked up, asking the ceiling to look after Andy. Poor man, always looking after her, when his own life was such a rat's nest. She believed she was helping him now by avoiding him, but since he knew her habits and hangouts, he could track her down in two minutes. To get her through last night, he had given his woman to another man. Pimped her out, as he might have said; degraded her so that she might live another day, and now she found she could not forgive him for that. Why did she permit him to do such things to them? Because he was bossy and she wished to be bossed. Her desire, or compulsion, to be so submissive may have been what enabled them to last so long together. How many temper tantrums had he thrown, and how many times had she walked away, saying she was sick of him and swearing never to speak to him again? How many? Too many. But like a battered dog, she stayed with him, or at least remained in skid row so that Andy, wishing to sweet-talk her back into his arms, could locate her without much effort. This time it's for real, she tells herself with what she believes is clarity of mind, firmness of purpose. She listens hard to these Gregorian hymns, as if expecting them to propel her into some sort of spiritual ecstasy. Listen to the music, her father had always told her. Each piece tells its own story. Maybe, he said, you will one day write your own masterpiece or two that will outlive you and a dozen generations of your progeny.

The mass began with the ringing of bells and the appearances of a priest and two altar boys. Annie, without a rosary and feeling the need to read something, reached over and picked up a copy of the New Testament. She stared at its ancient words with little comprehension and listened with one ear as the priest went on about that day's Lesson. Soon she closed the book and put it back. Why, she wanted to know, had so many people killed each other in the name of Christianity? She hadn't wondered about it in a long time, and now considered the question unanswerable and probably unimportant. Blinking away that thought, she gazed at an altar boy and mused that he might look like the love child she and Andy had never conceived. She watched as a woman, very old or perhaps just middle-aged but ground down from years of street life, kneel down before the priest, her gnarled hands covered with liver spots. After muttering a very quick prayer for the woman, Annie stood up and nearly fell over from lightheadedness. She wondered when she had last eaten, and decided to eat soon but couldn't think of what to eat or whether she could keep anything down. The church was filling up now, with Natives and some old Asians. One woman looked a bit like Annie's mum, who, of course, would never have gone into a church like this one. Her mum went to church to show off her fine clothes and impress everyone with her clever conversation. Annie and Andy always had it common: Both had no use for their mums.

Years after her father's suicide, Annie discovered his will among his personal papers, handwritten on a dimestore document when he surely knew he would kill himself soon. He had more assets than her mother said, and left most of them to Annie, who read the will and demanded an explanation. Her mother merely shrugged at having been found out.

Annie said: You robbed me of my Julliard education and musical career. Dad wanted *me* to have that money, Mum.

But her brother had gotten a Ph.D. and had a great

job, and there was something to be said for that. Annie didn't think she could find anyone who might empathize with her complaints. Annie stayed with her mother for a time but then moved out, leaving the old woman alone until she called her son the engineer, who deposited her into Bayporte's cheapest home for old folks, which was not cheap at all. He left her there in the care of the highly trained, personable staff whom she despised. She died, lonely and bitter, in the Bayporte Royal Care Center, or whatever they called it.

Too bad for you, Mum.

Oh, Annie! How could you be so callous? Weren't you young and self-reliant, too, for a little while? Now you're at the Pattison, staring at chipped plaster, peeling paint and bedclothes stained with God knows what. This just won't do for you, Annie, because you've had better everything than most other people can imagine. The groan and squeak of the Pattison's bedsprings, the strange and terrible people who have slept and fucked in this bed while you weren't in it! Awful!

The Pattison, of course, has no in-room telephone,

but Annie doesn't mind, because she has no one left to call. Her room has no clock, but she doesn't care about the time. What about a TV? No, and she's not interested in that brain-rotting appliance.

Naturally, she is deluding herself whenever she thinks that anyone cares about her many showers, lotions and powders. Years earlier, her men cared a great deal about Annie's personal hygiene, especially Gary, the owner of Hinman Music. Her former lover and employer, he had always been vain about his shaggy hair and goatee, and when she saw a man who looked like him, she became nostalgic for her days by his side on the wrong end of Grand Street. Gary had died some time ago and no longer had to endure the tedium of living; Annie envied him. At nineteen, she started working for him, selling and demonstrating pianos and guitars and harmonicas. Although trained in the classics, she insisted on playing popular music in the store, because that was the kind of music her customers liked and responded to emotionally. She even sang sometimes, her voice a heartbreakingly pure falsetto that made customers' eyes well up with tears.

Check her out as she plays *I Want to Know What Love Is*. As soon as she stops, a couple buys a piano so that the wife can learn to play that ballad, too. Gary personally takes their order and winks at his ace saleslady. Yea, Annie!

Then: Annie, pushing thirty, is still at Hinman Music. She wants to accuse Gary of stealing her best years, then realizes that he didn't have to steal them because she gave them to him. She will probably never marry—who could put up with her?—and fade away as just another frustrated old musician. Annie once in a while thinks of her instructors at Julliard, who really didn't get what *they* wanted, either.

On rainy days, business is slow at Hinman Music. The prostitutes and drug dealers who loiter in the area have no use for pianos and guitars. Also, the store carries so many big, heavy items that are a hassle to deliver, so they don't make a sale every day, but when they do, each one goes a long way towards paying their overhead. So Annie, during slow periods, sits at the piano and plays.

Did Gary wreck my life? She asks herself now.

Sure he did. I'll blame it all on him.

Hinman, not altogether falsely, often told his wife that he was working late at the store. To him, screwing Annie on his desk was part of his job. Afterwards, he talked shop. "I'm afraid," he said, catching his breath and zipping up his fly, "of losing my business. I'm afraid that someday soon they won't need me."

They really don't need you now, Annie wanted to say. She knew that Hinman Music, at the seedy end of the city's main drag, was a retail operation, not a cultural institution. Something else, Starbucks or whatever, would come along and replace it. Maybe the developers would knock it down and put up a highrise condominium.

Annie understood that. She did not understand why Gary would dump her for a bimbo he hired as a "saleslady" who could neither play instruments nor persuade customers to buy them. A bimbo, finally, who could not even keep the paperwork straight at the end of their business day.

Please don't go, Gary said to Annie. She's slow but she'll learn. You'll help me train her, OK?

So Annie, who cannot seem to say no to anyone, says OK.

She sits up straight in the church and admonishes herself to stop thinking about Gary Hinman. Mass is over, so she gets up and traipses down the street to the Good Luck Cafeteria for a cup of tea and a stale sweet roll. She drinks down all of the tea and wishes she hd more, but the sweet roll is too hard, and she's sure she would vomit if she forced herself to eat it. She gets up and heads for the public library, where they'll let her sit in one overheated area or another for hours at a time. Once there, she felt comforted by the library's warmth and promised herself she wouldn't fall asleep, but did anyway.

"Ma'am." She felt someone's gentle but firm hand on her shoulder. She looked up and saw a library staff member. "You can't sleep here. Read this." The woman dropped a copy of *The Canuck* into Annie's lap. Annie smiled up at her, grateful that the woman wasn't being a bitch. *The Canuck*'s front page was all about the World Winter Games. Most of Great Elizabeth, minus Annie and everyone else on skid row, considered the

Games a splendid happening. She forced herself to read, and the article said that the suits had gone to so much trouble over the Games and Bayporte would be in debt for years over it. Annie yawned and started thinking about hotel rooms. Would the Pattison have a vacancy for her? Of course; that flophouse always had a low occupancy rate.

If Annie and Andy had bought a house together, she is convinced that they would have become a stable, married couple. They were going to do exactly that while Andy had money and still believed in himself enough to overcome, or at least cope with, his personal demons. She believes that what he really needed was something tangible and substantial to call his own. Newly released from the Bullies, he went to work as a clerk at Haslett's Sports Collectibles, where he told Bullies stories and signed autographs. But then Haslett retired and offered to sell his business to Andy, who dreamed of renaming it Kennedy's Collectibles. But the bank wouldn't lend him the money, the store became a Denny's and Andy went on a month-long drunk.

"Nothin," he said, sobbing in Annie's arms, "ever goes right for me." Adding, "I keep gettin in my own way. I make everythin so hard for myself."

VI

Andy felt surprised when Pawlowski drove them all the way to skid row to pick up donations. What, he asked himself, did anyone have that they wanted to part with? And what did they have that someone else might want? But they stopped when they saw the fire down by the harbor. One of them old warehouses or other buildins musta finally got torched, Andy thought. Good riddance.

As Andy and Pawlowski stayed stuck in traffic, a huge explosion at the site of the fire thrusting chunks of blackened rooftop material into the sky and noxious clouds of smoke towards Andy and Pawlowski. The two men muttered curses as they rolled up their windows. A police officer appeared and pointed for them to return south. Pawlowski did so, muttering some more.

For lunch, the old man surprised Andy by giving him half a sandwich and half an apple. Andy thanked him and scarfed it down; he could have eaten three sandwiches and four apples and still had room for more.

"Won't go near the harbor today," Pawlowski said. "Too much smoke and traffic. Lots of other stops today in different parts of city." They drove to a section of Bayporte full of big old houses much like Pawlowski's and, at the old man's instruction, grabbed a crippled, rusted-out, wheel-less bicycle and hoisted it into the bed of the truck. As he wiped the rust from his hands to his pants leg, he saw Busker Rogers sitting on a three-legged desk.

Busker, now wearing a leather vest over a denim shirt and immaculate Levi's, smiled and nodded at Andy, who knew right away that Busker had been one of the casualties of the riot Andy started.

When the riot happened, I was downtown, playing my guitar, hoping for tips. But when the violence started, someone grabbed my guitar and hit me over the head with it. Gave me a concussion. Bleeding into the brain, you know. I ended up catatonic and my sister had to take care of me until I died. She made me into a poster child for riot casulaties.

"I remember when you died," Andy said to him. "I wanted to attend your funeral but your sister told me to get lost. She blamed me for what happened to you."

The Busker nodded. *She had to blame someone. It was just her nature. I didn't blame you. I was a grown man who had made a conscious decision to play guitar in a dangerous situation. Your problem, Andy, is that you're a kind man with evil hands that just won't obey you.*

Andy went back for more junk to cram into Pawlowski's truck. When he returned, he discovered Rob La Porte sitting on the desk alongside the Busker. Next to them were a couple of others Andy did not know by name but assumed were riot victims like the Busker.

"All done," Andy said to Pawlowski. "Let's take off."

"Hey? You in a hurry for someplace?"

"Naw, but we have plenty of stuff, so let's go."

Pawlowski rolled his eyes. "Homeless guy is restless to get going, like he has somewhere to go."

The two men climbed into the truck. Andy felt relieved to be away from those dead guys with their gaping head wounds. Andy took a deep breath and hugged himself against the cold. Pawlowski insisted on keeping his window open because he liked the feel of the frigid draft in his face. Andy looked down at his hands and studied them for the longest while. Were they, as he had been told, not *his* hands but an independent pair of living things intent on causing as much death and destruction as possible? I have remarkable hands, he said to himself. Athlete's hands with long fingers and broad palms. I could grip and manipulate a hockey stick so well because of my hands. They're still pretty good, even though they're startin to deteriorate, just like the rest of me.

I don't own these hands. Satan does, but somehow I got stuck with them.

"You got a problem?" Pawlowski asked him.

"Hey?"

"You got a problem with your hands? You keep staring at them."

"No problem. I wasn't just starin. I was admirin them."

"Admiring your hands? I didn't know people were

supposed to do that."

"Do you like your hands?" Andy asked him.

"Never thought about it. I got other parts of me I admire very much." Pawlowski chuckled. "Other people admire those parts of me, too."

"My hands," said Andy, "are lethal weapons."

"That so?"

"My hands are more interestin than lots of people I've met."

"Whatever." Pawlowski turned on the radio.

Andy felt puzzled about his fascination with his own hands. He had also felt, many times over the years, such distress and desperation that he dared himself to attempt suicide. How often had he awakened under a bridge or in the weeds in a familiar city like Bayporte or an unfamiliar one like Pittsburgh, hung over and hopeless, frozen as a cake of ice, and said to himself: Andy, you don't want to go through that ever again, do you? It's just not worth it. Next time will be even worse. Don't be a bloody coward. There's the bridge. Just do it.

But no. You lay there for close to an hour, feelin

sorry for yourself and sayin that life's not worth livin. Then you get up, wipe the frost off and scrounge up some change for coffee. You forget all about the bridge.

Andy's suicidal ideations confused him, just as he found himself unable to comprehend his inability to end his own life even when it became clear that his prime had long since ended and his future was full of difficult things that would only get worse. He had eschewed, each day, many opportunities to do himself in, and nodded with much empathy as Annie told him of her father's suicide following his financial devastation. But Andy was different; he kept himself busy trying to survive each day, and that became his life's work. He wasn't the kind just to lay down and die. Shit, man, that was too easy.

Truthfully, he had never thought of himself as the kind to flee from trouble, but that was exactly what he had done for years, whenever things got bad. Who would have thought that Andy's mum, during Thanksgiving dinner, would tell everyone at the table that Andy and his mousy little lower-class new wife

Carroll would no longer be permitted inside the Kennedys' Fairview Avenue home. ("Lower class"! As if the Fairview Avenue Kennedys were Canadian aristocrats!) The old lady thawed out a bit after a few years and let Andy in but still barred his working-poor little wife even as the two stood knocking at her door. Andy's relationship ended with them ended then until his mother died.

Run.

Flee. Not for the first time, and hardly for the last.

He took off after killing the cop.

He went again as a member of the Bullies, his life a whirlwind of airline trips, buses, taxis, hotel rooms and arenas. Those hours in distant cities, playing before crowds who loved him despite themselves. He liked it all.

He loved a dozen things, and liked a hundred more, about Bayporte.

But then, inevitably, it's autumn again.

Won't be long before the snow starts fallin, but it in Bayporte it's usually just rain, rain, rain.

It's hockey time, and Andy gets itchy feet.

He stuffs his gear into his bag and says, Bye.

...

Pawlowski stopped or donations at a house near Oliver Johnson Secondary School, which Andy had attended in the 1970s. He watched as a vast number of teenagers wearing parkas and carrying knapsacks exited the school, their faces white, black, brown and yellow. Mostly brown and yellow, he thought. Plenty of Pakis and Chinks when he went there, but back then they didn't own the neighborhood. Mum didn't mind the colored people all that much, as long as there weren't too many of them and they didn't move next door to her. Andy's friend Hank Adamski went twice a week to receive further instruction on how to be a good Catholic and learn the ways of pleasing God. Andy, an indifferent Protestant mainly concerned with finding ways of pleasing himself, spent his afternoons with copies of *Playboy* magazine.

In Pawlowski's truck, Andy shuddered at the thought of Tom and Diane and their white house, a few blocks away, that once had been his, too. He recalled his most recent conversation with Tom, who insisted he come over for dinner. I'll bring a turkey, said Andy. Fuck that, said Tom, just bring yourself.

Pawlowski bounded back into the truck and shook his head. "That guy just now? He wanted me to take away his shit. I don't want shit, I want junk. Some people don't know the difference between shit and junk." He pulled out onto the street and Andy tried to picture going home for Sunday dinner. How to do it? Just knock on the door, smile and say what? 'Hidy, it's me'? He'd feel like a fuckin fool, standin there at *their* door, which used to be *his* door, too. And them standin there, pretendin he wasn't a drunken bum who'd spent years runnin away from life's challenges.

"Let me off at the end of the street," he told Pawlowski. "It's Miller time, eh? I'm beat."

"We quite when I say so," replied Pawlowski.

"No. I know some people out this way and I wanna say hi."

"So get out and see your friends."

"You owe me money," Andy told him.

"I don't know how much. I need to figure it out. Come see tomorrow and I'll pay you."

Andy shook his head. "I worked most of the day. I'm tired. I want my money now."

"I'll pay you thirty-five dollars. Half day's work."

"No, sir. Sixty is what we agreed on, but I'll settle for fifty. You gave me next to nothin for lunch. I'm starvin."

"I am boss. I say thirty-five."

"I'm not leavin without fifty. You're a big man, but I'm no weaklin either, and I played hockey for years. I'm not let you rip me off. I've punched out lots of guys over these kinds of disputes. You followin me, guy?"

The big old man looked at Andy for a few seconds, then looked away. "I do you favor by hirin you when no one else will, and you threaten me with physical violence. Thirty-five is what I said."

"And *I* said I'm not leavin without fifty dollars in my hand." Then, "You know what thirty-five dollars buys? It don't even buy thirty-four dollars?"

Pawlowski sighed and shrugged. He pulled out a red polymer Canadian fifty-dollar bill and handed it to Andy. Good old Canadian money, every color of the rainbow, he thought as he pocketed the banknote.

"Thanks very much, Mr. Pawlowski," said Andy.

"Get out of here, you drunken bum," said Pawlowski. Go back to skid row and drink yourself to death. I don't like your kind."

"Sorry to hear that. I'm not such a bad guy, once you get to know me a bit." Andy jumped out of the truck and waved goodbye to Pawlowski, who drove off in a hurry.

...

Andy walked along Fairview Avenue, feeling stiffer than he could ever remember. Each step required some effort and a few deep breaths. Good thing I was never much of a smoker, he said to himself as he traipsed along. A middle-aged woman stepped onto the sidewalk just ahead of him.

"Excuse me," Andy said, "do you know where I could buy a turkey?"

The woman turned around, frowning, and blanched when she saw the slovenly man who'd spoken to her. "Hey?"

"I said—"

The woman hurried back into her house and a man came out. "What did you say to my wife?"

"I asked her where I could buy a turkey," Andy said.

"Why do you want a turkey?"

"Because," Andy said, "I'm lonely, I need a friend I can talk to."

"Take off, guy."

"I hear ya." Andy moved on. Soon he encountered a group of boys and asked them about a turkey.

"Yeah," said one. "Fairview Meats at Forty-ninth."

Andy laughed. "Is that bloody place still open?" He thanked the boys and headed up to Forty-ninth. The stores and their signs were largely unfamiliar to him, and the experience made him feel as if he were in some eastern Canadian or American city and was happily ignorant of its layout, culture and secrets. He thought of a plump, fresh turkey in a big clear window and walked faster. Would he settle for anything less than a turkey? No. As always, he wanted what he wanted.

At the the corner of Fairview Avenue and Forty-ninth Street, Andy felt better. Fairview Meats, decades old, looked brand new, floored in dark wood—not that plastic stuff that was supposed to look like wood, Andy observed—and spotless everywhere. Its front-window display case featured every kind of meat.

"I'd like a turkey," Andy told the young woman in her clean white apron.

"I can help you with that," she replied. "How big a bird would you like?"

"Fifty bucks' worth."

"That'll get you a fifteen-pounder."

"Good enough."

As she wrapped it, he asked, "How's business?"

She frowned. "Bad. You're the only one here. This neighborhood has gone to the Indians, Chinese and Vietnamese. They don't eat what we eat."

Andy shrugged. "People food is people food, right?" Then, "You got this place clean as a hospital. I could eat right off the floor."

"If it was grimy, we'd be out of business." She smiled. "Enjoy your turkey. Don't eat it all at once or you'll puke."

. . .

He walked down Fairview Avenue to Forty-first Street and looked north at the magnificent mountain range that hulked over downtown Bayporte's skyline. Across the street, Oliver Johnson Secondary School looked very much as it had when Andy attended it so many years earlier. The stores have all changed, Andy thought, and the people I knew have moved, but it's still good ol Fairview, hustlin and bustlin. Maybe *I'm* the thing that's changed so much.

In the cold weather, the turkey stayed fresh in Andy's arms. He kept walking down Fairview, grateful that it was all downhill from here. As he got closer to his destination, he told himself, Betcha they'll think I want them to cook the bird now and serve it to me for supper, and I wouldn't say they were wrong.

At the Kennedys' front door, he felt his legs weakening. The turkey felt almost leaden in his arms. Gettin too old for these walks. He looked around, saw nobody, then looked down at the turkey and thought, Just you and me, kid. We just gonna stand around here and do nothin? He stared at the white house that, for so long, he had called home. Then he pushed the button and heard the bell ring from inside. He could hear the hurried, hushed steps and felt an eyeball checking him out through the peephole. Then the door opened a bit.

"Hey." They don't know who I am. Is that good or bad?

"Who are you?"

"I'm me. Brought ya somethin to eat." He jiggled the turkey.

"Excuse me?"

"I brought ya a turkey. I told Tom I would be by one of these days. Well, today's that day."

The door swung wide open. The blonde woman stood before him, her eyes as wide as saucers. "Andy! Is it really you?"

He smiled. "Don't much look like me, hey, Carroll?"

She shook her head. "Oh wow. Oh wow."

"Mind if I come in?"

Inside, they went into the kitchen and Carroll put the turkey on the stove while they talked. "You know," she said, "we read that story about you. It was online."

He grinned. "I hope you didn't feel too humiliated."

She laughed. "Not at all. We thought it was funny. The Bayporte police are something, hey? Arresting a man just for using the ladies' washroom."

"I had a good lawyer. He saved me from lethal injection."

Carroll laughed again. "Oh, Andy! It's just *so* good to see you again!" She pointed at the turkey. "You really didn't have to bring anything."

"A wise man once said, 'If you come a-callin, make sure you don't show up empty-handed.'"

Andy, looking at Carroll, felt pleased that she still had her natural teeth and they hadn't gotten dingy. He couldn't tell if her hair was blonde or gray; she'd never been the type to color her hair or paint her face, anyway. Her breasts had sagged a bit, but her belly and bum were still where they were supposed to be, thanks to a metabolism that kept her thin; he couldn't remember many times when she had turned down goodies. Still, he could see that the life of a homemaker had ground her down, but who was *he* to criticize *her*?

The way she was at Fast Eddie's years ago.

The tough guys who frequented that place said she was the prettiest girl around. They said that about all the cuties.

But in Carroll's case, they were right.

She'd gone in there looking for Fast Eddie.

Andy saw her and worked up more nerve than he thought he had. He went up to her and introduced himself.

'How's it goin, eh?' he'd said.

By the end of the evening, they were sitting together, holding hands and he spoke the corniest, most unhip bullshit to her.

And they kissed. A lot.

Later on, he would compare Carroll's kisses to Rikia's, and conclude that, as kissers, the two women had nothing in common. Looking now at Carroll, who couldn't get the smile off her face, he decided that kisses were funny things that said a lot more than we knew. They come from different parts of us and travel to different parts of the other person. The kisses from the head are too mental and don't mean as much as they should. Kisses that come from the heart are like hugs that convey empathy but lack passion. Kisses that come from the groin feel great while they're happening, but like a silly movie or a plate of Chinese food, we forget about them an hour later. But kisses that come from all three places—the head, heart and groin, the way Rikia's did—well, you couldn't forget *those* ones even if you wanted to, and you'll probably spend the rest of your life looking for more of them.

Carroll's first kisses meant so much to him.

He married her not long afterwards.

Rikia, I will remember your kisses forever.

But you belonged to someone else, and now I do, too.

...

"It's a wonderful turkey," Carroll said. "I can cook it now and we'll have it for supper."

Andy shook his head. "It'll take forever. You can just put it in the freezer and have it some other time."

"It wouldn't take so long. Anyway, I don't want you

to go buggering off so soon. You just got here and you've been away for so long."

"I'm not just buggerin off."

"Then just sit and wait while I get to work on this bird. Diane can peel some vegetables and Calvin can go to the bakery and get a pumpkin pie." She sighed and ran a hand through her hair. "You and a turkey. I wasn't expecting this."

"Who's Calvin?" Andy asked.

Carroll stopped and thought for a moment. "Your grandson. Diane married Brian Westmacott. You remember Brian, don't you? They have a son, Calvin. He'll be eleven soon."

"I," Andy muttered, "have an eleven-year-old grandson I didn't even know about."

Carroll nodded and smiled. "Tall as a tree and smart as a whip."

"Elisa," he said. "She would be in her twenties now."

"Yes."

"She's buried across the street. I went to her grave yesterday."

Carroll's eyes grew wide. "Really?"

"Yeah. I figured out where she was and talked to her."

"Talked to her."

"I told her what was goin on," Andy said. "Or maybe I was just talkin to myself. I don't much believe in talkin to dead folks."

Carroll chuckled. "Same old Andy. Well, I hope you at least felt better after talking."

He shrugged. "Could be. Say, where's Tom?"

"Taking a nap. He's got so much happening right now that he barely has time to breathe. Let me wake him up so he can at least say hello."

Andy shook his head. "No, let him get his beauty sleep. You and I can just sit here and talk some more."

"We have so much to say. I don't know where to start."

Andy's eyes took in the whole kitchen. "Place kinda is the way I remember it. So is Oliver Johnson School. But up the hill, when I went to get the turkey, all the old stores are gone, except for Fairview Meats."

Carroll nodded. "Yes, the old stores are gone. Is

that a bad thing?"

"I think so. Of course, no one consulted me when they closed those stores." Then, "How are your people? Your brothers and sisters? Everyone gettin by all right?"

"Clair is still Clair, still working at City Hall. Louise has gained weight and lost hair. Maggie got married, but two years later her husband dropped dead, so she's feeling very sorry for herself and doesn't leave her apartment too often. But we all talk to each other."

"Tom's doin OK, eh?"

"Yes and no. He has quite a gambling problem. He goes to Reno or Las Vegas every other weekend and comes back broke."

"Addictive personality, eh? I wonder who he gets that from. He was nice to come downtown and help me out that time. He gave me money but I drank it all away. He's a good kid. He told me that after Elisa died, you didn't tell anyone about how she died."

"It was nobody's business," said Carroll.

"You," Andy told her, "are some kind of special woman."

"Elisa's death was just one of life's tragedies. Wasn't anyone's fault. We need to put it behind us and take advantage of whatever time we have left." She looked closely at him. "So, end the suspense. Why *did* you come back to see us?"

"I suppose," Andy replied, "that it was Tom's invite and me thinkin that one of these days I'm gonna come by. But that wouldn't be the only reason. Every day and night, I live among people who don't have nothin or no one and I know that here I have people who value me. So I guess that's the real reason I'm here right now."

"You're a different man now, Andy," Carroll said. "Tom says you have a new wife. He met her and said her name is Annie."

Andy shook his head. "Not married. Just hangin out together. You're the only wife I ever had or wanted."

Carroll smiled, but Andy thought that there were as many smiles as kisses, and each one had a very different meaning. He didn't know what Carroll's smile meant. "I've only had one husband," she said. "I've only been with one man."

Andy sat there, not knowing what to say.

"Too bad for you," he finally said.

"Not too bad. I wanted it that way."

"You musta had offers."

She nodded. "But I said no. I went out with family and friends. I didn't date because I felt I was already someone's girl and I didn't believe in cheating."

"I couldn't have got married again because I'm pretty sure you and I are still married and I was damned if I was gonna divorce you. But there's Annie, and I won't lie about it. We were together for years, except for the times when I was drinkin and she got fed up and told me to piss off till she cooled off and then we'd get back together again. Annie, she came from a rich family, she studied music at Julliard, but she don't have enough sense to come in out of the rain. I'm not exaggeratin. I'm afraid of what might happen to her if I wasn't around all the time lookin out for her."

Carroll listened with a neutral expression as her husband told her of his many years of marital infidelity. "Where is Annie?"

He shrugged. "Haven't seen her lately. If we get separated, we usually meet up at the mission. One of these days, she's gonna stumble out into the street and get squashed by a bus or somethin."

"You and she are together for a reason," Carroll said.

"Yeah, so she won't get squashed by a bus."

"Do *you* need *her*?"

"No." He paused. "Yes. I'd like to think that I don't, but I guess I need to make myself useful, and if somethin tragic happened to her, I couldn't forgive myself."

"What do you need, Andy, at this time of your life? To make you happy."

"Nothin much. I'm pretty self-reliant. I can get myself together to do a day's work whenever I can find someone who's desperate enough to hire me. I still have plenty of good memories to make me feel good. Do you remember us makin out in Fast Eddie's joint?"

Carroll smiled. "Such a long time ago."

"Dammit, Carroll," said Andy, fighting back tears,

"I've missed you and the life we had together. The only time I was ever good for anythin was when I was young and could play hockey. But even that meant nothin compared to havin a family and cookin a meal and doin all the other things normal people do. I tried to bathe my baby girl and couldn't even do that right. Just about everythin I ever touched turned to shit, so I learned to run away from problems, and I got pretty good at that. I guess I ended up in skid row because I thought I deserved to be there as punishment. Carroll, I've seen things and done things you don't ever want to know about. We have so much to say to each other, but maybe we'll never say it all because it's just too awful. But you need to believe me when I say that no matter where I was or what I was doin, I always loved you and the kids and thought about what was and what could be. I don't want your prayers or pity. I just want you to know that I've always felt that you and the kids were mine and I was yours. No matter where I was, in Montreal or California or Florida, I always felt that Bayporte was my home and you were my family. Now, after sayin all that, I'm ready to starve to death.

How would you feel about fixin me a sandwich and a cup of tea?"

. . .

After Andy had his say, neither of them spoke for quite some time until, finally, Carroll got up and started to prepare the turkey. She made some of those most trivial conversation Andy had ever heard outside of skid row. He looked out the big window and marveled at how little their front yard had changed. The section of Fairview Avenue on which his father's gory death had occurred remained the same dark-gray, well-traveled roadway it had always been.

Andy felt the urge to flee, but this time it was up, not out. The boneyard, as always, made him feel envious of those people who were no longer *people*, precisely, but perhaps something better. His father, who had told him to enjoy life and stay young, had, in Andy's mind, taken his own advice. On Fairview Avenue, as the sedan sheared off his leg and he died, did his soul—or spirit, or whatever was at his core— fly off to some stellar paradise, or did that tiny flame— as Andy himself pictured the life-force—that had made him *him* just flicker out as if it never existed? Andy, of course, wanted to believe in angels, heaven and life after death and all the rest of that too-good-to-be-true stuff that grownups told little kids to make them shut up. But he always concluded that death was a long, deep sleep. If death was "nothing," he had "nothing" to worry about. Then how come he worried about it so often?

. . .

Carroll busied herself setting the dinner table with a crisp tablecloth. She took out the silverware that Andy recognized as a wedding gift from Fast Eddie. He heard the door open and close, then he saw Calvin Westmacott bounce into the front room after dropping his knapsack in the hallway. He frowned at the sight of Andy.

"How's it goin?" his grandfather asked.

"Calvin," said Carroll, "this is your grandfather. He's come for dinner."

Calvin nodded and tentatively shook Andy's outstretched hand. "Hello, sir."

Andy smiled. "Glad to meet ya, Calvin. You're big

for your age, hey? Just gettin home from school, I guess."

"Are you a Kennedy or a Westmacott?" he asked.

"He's your Grandpa Kennedy," Carroll explained. "His name is Andrew Carson Kennedy."

Andy laughed. "That's a mouthful, eh? I haven't heard my full name in years."

"You were a hockey player, right?" Calvin asked him. "You played for the Bullies. Is that what happened to your teeth?"

"Calvin—"

"No, that's all right," Andy said, waving Carroll off. "I lost some while playin hockey, and lost some more later on. But I still got a few."

"Tom says you taught him lots about hockey," Calvin said. "Can you teach me, too?"

Andy nodded. "A long time ago I got Tom on the ice and showed him a few things, but I'll see if I can do that for you. What's your position?"

"Center," he said. "Just like Gretzky."

"You're a big boy. Gonna be a big man, too, I guess. Gretzky was small, but he was the exception.

Also, he had bigger guys protectin him."

"There's a trunk in the attic, you know," Calvin told him. "It had your hockey stuff in it. Is there an autographed picture of Gretzky in there, too?"

"Colton," Carroll asked, "why were you in that trunk? It's none of your business."

"Tom and I went through it together," Calvin said. "There's no girlie magazines in there."

"You should have a look in that trunk," Carroll said to Andy.

"Maybe I will."

Carroll led them towards the spare bedroom. Calvin ran ahead of them and shouted, "Tom! Wakey-wakey! WE got company!"

Suddenly they saw Tom standing in the doorway. He was wearing his robe and his hair stuck out in every direction. He yawned and rubbed his eyes.

"How's everythin, Tom?" Andy said.

"It's all good. Glad to see you finally took me up on my invite."

"Surprised ya, eh?"

Tom nodded and grinned. "Yeah, but it's a good

surprise."

"He brought us a turkey," Carroll said. "We're having it for supper."

"I'm due downtown tonight," Tom said. "We have a meeting for a progress report on Rash Singh's chances for becoming the next premier of Great Elizabeth."

"How's that comin along?" Andy asked.

Tom shrugged. "I think everyone's warming up to the idea of having Rash as premier. But if he doesn't get in, they'll all blame *me*. Especially Rash."

Andy chuckled, but then he smelled his own stench. While it wasn't as bad as it had been, it seemed to be getting worse by the moment. Down on skid row he didn't notice such things very often because he usually smelled no worse, and frequently much better, than the other bums. Also, he had such a low regard for those bums, and they for him, that if his stink offended him, well, that was just too bloody bad for them. But now, amongst his own, he decided that his reek wouldn't do.

"Tom," Carroll said, "you can't go out just yet

because your father is here for dinner. Also, we're going up to the attic to look at this things in the trunk."

"As I recall," said Andy, "you like turkey."

"And as I'm sure *you* recall," Tom retorted, "I've never met a food I didn't like." Then, "You want to get a quick shave? You can use my electric razor."

"Tom," Carroll said, "don't start bossin him around. Get your clothes on and join us in the kitchen."

Andy and Carroll then went up to the attic.

...

Andy smiled at the sight of the battered old trunk that contained the only tangible evidence that Andy Kennedy, at least as he saw it, had ever amounted to anything. Opening the lid, he felt puffs of dust slap his face like the hand of lost decades and unfulfilled promise. Looking down, he saw, right away, a splendidly handsome young man with smiling eyes and a half-serious mouth. The teenaged, or young adult, Andy Kennedy, frozen forever in a photograph. In the trunk, around and underneath the picture, were pieces of hockey apparel and a Canadian flag. About half a dozen pictures of Andy sat in the trunk, showed him with wavy, mussed-up hair, plenty of teeth and a mostly no-bullshit countenance. To avoid concussions, he had always worn his helmet; alas, over time he had taken his share of punches and sticks to the face and spat out some of his teeth. He paid particular attention to one picture of himself, surrounded by teammates, all of them in full uniform. The picture was unremarkable except for the fact that, just a moment before the photographer snapped the shutter, one of the players tossed a puck into the air, and there it sat suspended, forever resisting gravity and the other forces of nature. To Andy, the puck in the air, and his own handsome young face looking back at him, made the impossible possible. The puck had stayed up there for decades; Andy could look like a kid forever. So why couldn't he start to defy gravity, or nature, or God, or whatever had reduced him to alcoholic homelessness? Hadn't he done the impossible by making his way home, with a turkey, and coming full circle up here in the attic?

The puck stays up there. Nothing can bring it down.

Can't Andy say the same for himself?

Andy's sure that Calvin notices his grandfather's missing teeth. He's probably thinkin: Can't the old man buy himself some new ones? People do it all the time.

...

Andy went through all the contents of the trunk and found his skates and gloves, plus a couple of suits and a pair of black dress shoes. He also discovered shirts and underwear. Finally, he picked up a puck and had a long look at it. "Bobby Orr. Forgot all about it."

"Whatcha got there?" Calvin asked.

Andy handed it to him. "A puck signed by Bobby Orr. Don't touch the signature. It might get smudged."

"Bobby who?"

"Bobby Orr. In his own way, he was as good as Gretzky, if you ask me."

Carroll pointed at the two-piece suit Andy had taken out, a three-button, dark-gray pinstriped outfit with pleated slacks and wide lapels. "I remember," she said, "when you bought that suit. You went to the most exclusive men's store in Bayporte and said, 'I want the most expensive suit you have.' You came home with it and I almost made you take it back. I still think it's the ugliest thing I've ever seen."

Andy laughed. "I had more money than brains. I wonder if it'll still fit."

"You have plenty of clothing in there. Put together an outfit, then take a shower and change into these clean things."

He nodded. "Good idea. I know the way." He gathered up a bundle of clothes and went downstairs to the washroom. Holding up the suit for closer inspection, he thought: She's right' it is ugly. I was a fool to buy it in the first place. Might as well wear it myself now, because if I gave it to the Sally Ann, they probably couldn't get two bucks for it. The Sally Ann would probably shit, too, if they knew how much I paid for the suit back then. He tried on the shoes, bought at the same time as the suit and at four times the price he had ever paid for footwear, and found them as gleaming, sleek and uncomfortable as ever.

Then he stripped naked, stepped into the shower and turned on the water.

After ten or fifteen minutes, he toweled off, used Tom's electric shaver and looked out the window. He saw Marco Rigoni, Rob LaPorte and Rockin Rod Brollar building stands in the back yard.

...

Andy Kennedy, that man about town, came into the living room wearing a maroon tie, solid white shirt, funky gray suit and gleaming black shoes. His entire outfit looked so outdated that Andy, with his hair parted in the center, could have passed for one of Al Capone's boys. So here I am, he said to himself, the best-dressed, most immaculately groomed wino in all of Canada.

"Damn," said Tom, looking up at him from the dinner table.

"Wow," said Carroll.

"Weird clothes," said Calvin.

Andy chuckled. "The gang downtown is probably gonna laugh at me, but so what." He added, "I left the old stuff in a heap in the washroom. The Sally Ann might have some use for it."

"Calvin will gather it all up and put it into garbage bags," said Carroll.

Tom looked at the pictures and newspaper clippings spread across the dining room table. "You weren't home very much," he said. "I didn't really know how good a player you were until I heard people, perfect strangers, bragging about you. Then I got on the ice and played, too, and I found out for myself how hard hockey was and how much talent you had. You were good, damn good."

Andy gave a little nod. "I had my moments."

"Those sports reporters couldn't stop gushing about you."

"I made them look good. I gave them long interviews and said more than I should have. I was a colorful character."

"Do you want to go outside and take a look at the back yard?" Carroll asked.

"Yeah," Andy said. "Be nice to get a breath of fresh air."

They went outside and sat on the steps. The sky

looked clear but the cold hadn't let up a bit. At least there was no rain or snow to complicate the lives of Andy's friends down on skid row.

"Do you," Carroll asked him, "have anywhere to stay tonight?"

"Yeah," he said, "I can find a dozen or more nooks and crannies downtown. That's never a problem."

"I thought," Carroll said, not looking at him although they were side by side, "that you could stay the night here, and tomorrow night and so on. Isn't that sort of why you're here?"

"Not exactly sure why I'm here. I don't think I could come back permanently. Too much has happened. We've all changed so much. It just wouldn't work out."

"I had just assumed you came by to give it a try."

"Might've crossed my mind, but it would be a bad idea. No can do."

"It would be difficult," Carroll conceded. "It would awkward at first."

Andy laughed. "It would be much more than just difficult and awkward."

"But we would get past that, and it would be as if you had never been gone."

"Kinda doubt that."

"I am amazed," she said, "that you went up to the cemetery and spoke to Elisa."

"Nothin amazin about it. I just went up to her gravestone and said what I had on my mind. That place is pretty. I didn't want to leave."

"That little section belongs to our family. There's a plot for you, one for me, a couple for the children. I guess Diane will want one for her kids, but I hope that's all years away."

"Got one for me too, hey?" Andy asked.

Carroll smiled. "Of course. You're one of us."

"There were lots of times when I didn't think I was. I figured you had no use for me, runnin off and all."

Carroll gave a small sigh. "Diane's been angry at you for the longest time. So was I, but now I figure we're all running out of time and I'm not going to hold grudges anymore. I imagine Diane will be quite frosty towards you at first, but she'll get over it."

"Maybe she won't. Maybe I should just shove off

so that nasty confrontation doesn't happen."

"The only thing worse than that confrontation," Carroll told him, "would be no confrontation. You two are father and daughter. That hasn't changed, and the greatest tragedy would be for the two of you never to speak to each other again. You need to have that confrontation and then get over it so that you can have a relationship again."

"As easy as that, eh? She's gonna say, 'Why did you leave us all alone?' and I'll be damned if I can give her a decent answer."

"Just tell her that you were a different person back then who couldn't cope with some of the things that happened. It's the truth, isn't it?" Then, "You know, Tom felt good when he found you downtown and you let him slip you some money. It meant a lot to him that he could help you in some way. He thought it meant that one day you might come back to us forever."

Andy grunted. "He's tryin to become a big political hotshot in this town, and his old man is a wino in skid row. Nice, eh?"

"Andy," Carroll asked, "why do you have to say such mean things about yourself?"

"Just bein honest. I *am* a mean person. I couldn't have survived in skid row for this long if I was nice."

The men had finished building the stands, and they, plus everyone else, started settling into them: Slick Willie James, Fast Eddie, the young Brian Westmacott and dozens of others Andy recognized from various epochs of his life but couldn't name at that particular moment.

You're all dead, so how come you're here, hauntin me? You belong in the cemetery across the street with the other stiffs.

You pretended you knew everythin and I knew nothin. Well, that's bullshit. You were as ignorant as I was.

You'd still be in that friggin trunk in the attic if I hadn't let you out. So get lost, hey? Go bug someone else.

"Mum!" Tom called from inside. "Diane's just getting home!"

"OK." Carroll turned to Andy. "Before we go

inside and deal with everything, do you have anything more to say to me?"

Andy shook his head. "Nope. Let's just go do it."

...

When Andy entered the kitchen and saw Diane at the stove, she had already put her apron on over her work apparel. He considered her outfit too ostentatious for an office job. She wore a burgundy silk blouse with a matching skirt and brown leather boots, clothing that Andy thought was meant for a younger woman with a better body. Diane had a generous bottom, a meager top and spindly legs. He hair was short, dark and shiny. He thought she was quite beautiful, and he felt enormously pleased to be her father.

"How's it goin, Diane?" he asked as she turned around and saw him.

"Surviving," she replied. Killers' eyes could not grow colder. "No thanks to you."

"I guess I deserve that," Andy said in a cheerful voice as he sat at the dinner table across from Tom.

"Cut him some slack," Tom said to Diane. "He just got here, and he brought us that turkey you're basting."

"He runs off for years," Diane retorted, "and then he just shows up one day, and you tell me to cut him some slack. No, I don't think so."

"For fuck's sake, sis, lighten up."

"I'm just speaking my mind," said Diane. "I'm just telling you how it is."

"Oh? Is that so?" asked Carroll. "Do you *really* know how it is?"

"Yes, I do. I'm not going to jump for joy and say, 'Oh, wonderful! Look who's back! Who care about what he did to us twenty years ago? Now we can pretend everything's fine and be a family again!' Well, forget *that* noise. I'm not forgiving or forgetting."

"No one's askin ya to forgive or forget," Andy told her.

"Why did you come here?" Diane asked.

Andy shrugged. "Just seemed like the right thing to do."

Diane let out a small, bitter laugh. "Did it really? Were you in some alley this morning, sleeping off a hangover, thinking, 'I think I'll go visit my family that I ran away from twenty years ago. Yeah, I'll go buy a puny turkey and bring it with me, and I'll knock on their door and say hi.' Is *that* your idea of 'the right thing to do'?"

"Nothin puny about that bloody turkey," Andy said.

"So why did you leave skid row? Did you finally get tired of going nowhere and being nothing? Are you here to exploit us and our family?"

"Not here to exploit no one or nothin," he said.

"He just came to say hello," Carroll explained. "He's not moving in. I invited him to do that, but he said no."

"Gee, that's nice," Diane said, her voice getting louder. "If he wanted to move back in, she would let him."

"Nothin to get crabby about," Andy said. "You want me to leave? I'm gone. I'm leavin right now."

"For real?" asked Diane.

"Damn right. I'm out the door right now."

"See ya."

"No one's going anywhere!" yelled Tom. "Diane,

quit being such a bitch!"

"I'm a bitch because my long-estranged father shows up and I'm not willing to welcome him back with open arms?" Diane scowled and stormed out of the kitchen.

"Angry lady," said Andy.

"Confused," said Tom. "In her own way, she's very happy to see you again. She just doesn't know how to deal with her feelings right now."

"She'll get over it and settle down," Carroll told them.

"I don't have a problem with her yellin and screamin," Andy said. "Down in skid row, I hear a lot worse than that every day."

"She went ballistic," Tom said, "and now she's gone to cool off."

"Where's Calvin?" Andy asked. "I hope he didn't hear any of that."

"He's in his bedroom, fiddling on his computer," Carroll told him. "Probably online, looking for love. I hope he isn't illegally downloading music or movies. There was a thing on TV about that. You can get into trouble."

Andy chuckled. "I don't think he was totally blown away by that Bobby Orr puck I gave him. He's all 'Gretzky, Gretzky, Gretzky,' like most of the kids. The NHL, NBA, football and baseball? They're all havin strikes and lockouts. I don't remember havin those problems when I played for the Bullies."

"Got to make a pit stop." Tom got up and headed for the washroom.

Andy watched him leave the room. "You raised a couple of toughies."

"It's in their genes," Carroll said. "They're half yours, so you're half to blame."

Andy nodded and looked out the window. The dead men had finished erecting the stands; everyone had crowded onto them and sat holding a lighter or lit match. The sight, far more vivid than any Cisco or Mad Dog hallucination, came from a part of his brain that Andy now realized he had no control over.

"Is something wrong?" Carroll asked him.

"No," replied Andy. "This too shall pass."

...

"Diane looked nice," Andy told Carroll. "Does she like her job?"

"Not really. But it pays the bills."

"What's she do?"

"She's an administrative assistant. She works at a biotech. Know what that is?"

Andy nodded. "Makes cancer drugs and whatnot. How many drugs have they made?"

Carroll laughed. "None. Plus, they pay fairly well, and yet they have no revenue. They've developed some sort of drug that helps get the chemo to the tumor faster, but Diane says they're just having an awful time getting the government—American or Canadian, maybe both—to approve this drug. The company has fancy parties and writes decent paychecks, but who knows how long that will last, considering they've never earned a dime?"

"Beautiful woman," Andy said. "Nasty temper."

"Years ago," said Tom, "she had an offer to pose for *Playboy*. Mum said no."

"Damn right," said Carroll.

"*Playboy*, hey?" Andy laughed. "Tell me more."

"This photographer," said Tom, "came up and started checking out our local women. So he sees Diane and gives her his cared. It's all totally legit, right? They wanted to fly her down to L.A. and do the photo shoot. But then Mum shot it all down."

Carroll shook her head. "I wasn't about to let them degrade my daughter in front of the whole world."

"I don't see how showing a beautiful woman in her birthday suit is degrading to anyone. You're just celebrating the human body," Tom said.

"Also," Carroll said, "I didn't like that guy we dealt with. I kept thinking about that other nice Canadian girl who went down there with stars in her eyes. She was going to pose nude, get movie offers and have the whole bloody world at her feet. So what happened to her? She ended up being murdered her husband, who then killed himself." She sighed. "Bunch of bloody maniacs down there."

"Apples and oranges, Mum," Tom said. "Dorothy Stratten was a different person and it was a different time. I just thought that *Playboy* could have gotten Diane a one-way ticket out of boring old Bayporte and a new life in sunny California."

"Maybe," Andy said, "that was the issue. Your mum wanted to keep her kids at home."

"Yes," said Carroll, "I'll admit that was part of it. I also hated the idea that she would move down to Los Angeles, of all places."

Andy nodded. "I've been to Los Angeles a zillion times. It's a crazy place. I don't think she missed out on anythin by sayin no to *Playboy*."

"Want a cigarette?" Tom asked Andy. "Player's Light OK?"

"Yeah."

Carroll checked the turkey while the two men blew streams of cigarette smoke at each other. After some time, Diane returned with a white box that Andy recognized from the bakery. "Pumpkin pie," she said to nobody in particular. "I know this is what you like," she said to Andy.

He smiled up at her. "Thanks. Wouldn't be a real turkey dinner without pumpkin pie for dessert."

She smiled back, and he could see that her fury had faded as quickly as it had begun. That one's up and down like a roller coaster, Andy said to himself. Her smile, though not one of those big, all-teeth-revealed jobs that the photographers always tried to coax from their models, gratified him just the same. This girl is moody, more like her old man than she knows.

"I've got somethin here." Andy held up a letter. "I wanna read it to you while supper's still cookin. I got this years and years ago, durin a road trip in the States."

He took out the letter, three or four sheets long, and read it. "'Dear Daddy: I wonder if you ever stop to think that back here in Bayporte you have a daughter who misses her daddy very much and wants to hear from him. A daughter who gets so lonely that she nearly ran away with the circus last week if there had been a circus. I am writing this letter because I was doing my science homework but some of the questions were so hard that I knew I would never understand them. You should have been here to help me. I don't know why I have to study science because it's boring and I don't want to be a doctor or scientist anyway. I hope you are playing good hockey and your legs and back don't hurt too much like Mum says they do.'"

"I don't remember writing that letter," Diane said.

"You were pretty young," Andy told her. "But you sounded so adult in that letter that I kept it. Funny how we keep some things and throw away the others."

"That is a good letter," Tom said. "Funny stuff in there."

"Funny stuff everywhere," said Andy. "You just need to know where to look."

Diane, wiping tears from her eyes, went up to Andy and hugged him hard. Then Brian Westmacott arrived home and, for the first time in a very long while, the whole Kennedy family sat down to dinner.

VII

"Do I," Joey asked Andy, "seem like a vagrant to you?"

"Kind of."

"I like 'vagrant' better than 'bum,'" he said. "It sounds less insultin than bum. Don't you think so?"

Andy shrugged. "It's all the same to me. Bum, vagrant, pauper, indigent. Just words. If people don't like who I am, fuck em."

"The people who call us bums," Joey told him, "just want to feel superior to someone."

"Joey, you're a goddamn good vagrant. You have nothing to be ashamed of. I've met many bad ones. You're a good one. Be proud of that."

Joey chuckled. "A good vagrant, eh? Didn't know there was such a thing, I thought we were all bad."

"Nope. Just good men doin their best with the bad cards they've been dealt."

Joey nodded. "We're survivors, I guess. Lots of

vagrants die from livin this way. I guess many of the tough old ones are dead and gone now."

"They're bein replaced by the new vagrants," Andy said. "You see this bloody economy? Too many guys and not enough work to go around. Not too hard to lose everythin you got. The young guys who lose everythin end up here, and they're too soft and spoiled to survive on the street.

"You and me," he said, "we're tougher than the rest."

"'Tougher than the rest.'" Joey laughed. "Damn, Andy, I like that."

The two men walked towards the Ballantyne Hotel on another clear, starry but dreadfully cold Bayporte night. Andy, after eating dinner with his family, had ridden the bus downtown and hurried over to the mission in search of Annie. Instead, he found Big Red sitting alone, sipping stale coffee.

"Haven't seen Annie," Big Red said. "But Joey was over here not long ago, asking about you. He's either at the train station trying to get warm or he's squatting in one of those old houses by the harbor. But I guess you already know that." His face darkened. "Look, Andy, the cops are really clamping down on homeless people because of the bloody World Winter Games. The organizers are scared to death that the TV cameras will show pictures of people laying in the street or whatnot and the world will then know that Bayporte has social problems. The cops have been busting up homeless encampments and thrown the people in jail until after the Games."

Andy sighed. "Don't know why they have to be so rough on us. We're harmless. We just want to get high and then sleep it off."

"It's just because of the Games. After a couple of weeks, things will get back to normal."

Andy went to the old house by the harbor first. He knew that Joey liked that squat the most. Pushing open the house's crumbling door, Andy stepped inside and right away could smell the rot and reek. The place seemed scarcely less cold than outside, but at least the bums had a roof to protect them from the rain and snow. He listened for the scraping sound of rats' claws on wood, could near none but knew that the little critters were there anyway. Hope I don't step into any doo-doo or wee-wee, Andy thought as he groped his way a bit more into the house. He knew Joey would be safe here; the cops would never enter such a smelly place and risk getting their uniforms soiled.

Nearby streetlights cast slivers of light into the house, illuminating wadded-up newspapers and candy wrappers. Andy also saw some empty Cisco bottles and at least one man curled up in the fetal position. Walking past the sleeping man, Andy entered the next room and smiled at the familiar figure he saw sleeping there.

"Joey. Wake up. It's me, Andy. I've come to kiss you goodnight."

Joey sat up and rubbed his eyes. "Andy—?"

"Big Red said you were lonely, so I've come by to keep you company."

"I got nowhere to go, Andy. No money, no Cisco, no nothin. I thought of throwin myself off the Tyson River Bridge. I'd be doin the world a favor." He burst into tears and wiped his nose on the sleeve of his coat.

Andy grabbed Joey's arm and pulled him to his

feet. "You're not throwin yourself off no bridge. It's not your time yet. You need to stay tough and just keep on goin till it *is* time." He paused. "I've been lookin for Annie. Any idea where she is? I hate the thought of her wanderin around alone on these cold nights."

"Maybe," said Joey, "she got a decent flop on her own and you don't got to worry about her."

"Hope so. Anyway, let's get out of here and get a decent flop for ourselves."

"What's wrong with right here? It's free."

"But the cops might come in and drag us off to jail," Andy said.

"What's wrong with jail? You get three hots and a cot, and they let you out in a few months, when the weather is better."

Andy shuddered. "Jail? No thanks. No way. Andy Kennedy don't like jail and it don't like him."

The two men headed back towards skid row because Andy now believed that Annie, as Joey suggested, might have found a place to stay for the night, like the Pattison Hotel; they had her suitcase and she wanted it back. Or maybe Annie had been telling the truth about having a well-off brother who wanted to take her in.

"Where we goin?" asked Joey.

"To find Annie, so we three can live happily ever after."

"Andy, how come you always say things like that?"

"Because," Andy replied, "I am a romantic person."

...

Andy and Joey arrived at the Pattison Hotel just as Stelfox, the evening desk clerk, started closing out his paperwork for the night clerk.

"Stelly," said Andy, "has Annie been by?"

"Yeah, she's checked in. Her usual room. Seemed to be in good spirits." Stelfox signed this form and dated that one; Andy grinned at all the paperwork it took to run a third-rate place like the Pattison. Wouldn't it be a bit better, he wondered, if the Pakis or Chinks who owned the Pattison got computers like everyone else?

Andy took out two twenties and handed them to

Stelfox. "Give these to her and tell her to get some breakfast. Promise?"

"Yeah. Anything for Annie." He pocketed the cash.

"Tell her I'll come by later. Go up now and ask if she needs anythin, but don't tell her I sent you. Go do that now."

Stelfox, intimidated by the former Bully, nodded, locked his cash drawer and left. Minutes later, he cam back down. "Annie didn't open the door said she's fine, she don't need nothin but thanks for askin."

"All right," Andy said. "When she comes down, give her the cash and tell her we'll hook up at the mission the way we always do. You give her back her suitcase?"

"Yeah, she's got it. She paid for three nights, you know."

"That right, eh?" Andy chuckled. "Old gal has more money than I do."

Andy and Joey walked fast up the street. Joey asked, "OK, boss, what's the next stop? There's not much to do at this late hour."

"We're goin to see a nice fella who has a kind of

after-hours liquor store. Not many people know about it. He's gonna sell us some liquid crack."

Joey guffawed. "For real?"

"Joey, would I lie to you?"

Presently they arrived at an apartment building. "You wait here," Andy said. He pressed the buzzer, went inside and within minutes returned with a brown bag.

"Got two bottles of Cisco and one bottle of Mad Dog," he said. "Not exactly as tasty as a glass of Canadian Comfort over ice, but it'll do."

Right there on the street, Andy handed Joey a bottle of Cisco and took out another one for himself. They opened the bottles and chugged down the syrupy, fortified wine as if it were lemonade.

...

They ended up at a dingy place called Mrs. Johnson's, owned and operated by a tiny old woman with a mean smile. She accepted their cash and let them come in out of the cold.

"Hi Mum," Joey said.

"I'm not your mum. I'm Mrs. Johnson."

"I was just jokin."

"No jokes here. The only ones who call me Mum are the crazies and weirdos from the nuthouse. They don't know any better."

"OK, cutie," said Andy. "You like that, right? Every woman likes being called a cutie. Well, we need two beds."

Mrs. Johnson led them into a huge room with a dozen or more paper-thin, soiled mattresses.

"Fresh and lovely," said Andy as he surveyed the room. "Maybe I'll move in here forever."

"If your friend don't like it," Mrs. Johnson told Joey, "he can leave and freeze to death."

"I said it was fresh and lovely." Andy sat on one of the cots. Next to him, a man lay snoring. Andy gave him a hard shake and said, "Hey, wake up. I got some Cisco. Want a taste?"

The man rolled over, opened his eyes and nodded.

"I'll be damned," Andy said. "It's Saskatchewan Sal."

"Yeah, Andy, it's me."

"How come you go by Saskatchewan Sal?" asked

Joey.

"Because," said Sal, "I can't remember my last name."

"This here's my pal Joey," said Andy. "He's a few cents short of a dollar, but he's a good guy."

"You lookin good, Andy," said Sal. "Normally you the scruffiest thing on skid row, but right now you got a shave, fresh clothes and a bottle of booze. Where'd you get the money for that? you been sellin crystal meth or somethin?"

"Andy got the Cisco from a nice fella he knows," Joey said. "Andy knows lots of nice fellas."

Andy got up, took out his bottle of Cisco Berry and handed it to Sal, who took a long drink before handing it back. "That shit tastes worse than cough medicine, guy."

Andy smirked. "Not supposed to taste good. It's just supposed to get you pissed out of your tree."

"So how come you woke me up?"

"Just wanted to give you some bum wine before all the bums drank it all."

"Nice and dark in here," Sal said. "If I didn't feel so

damn cold all the time, I'd say I was better than all right."

"Tell me about it," said Andy. "I'm cold even with this parka on. The old lady here could turn up the heat a bit and I wouldn't mind, but she's probably too bloody cheap for that. good thing we got this Cisco to help us keep warm. Here, have another drink."

Sal nodded and accepted the bottle. He stared at its label. "Cisco Berry. Yuck. Andy, I thought you liked to drink Canadian Comfort."

Andy chuckled. "I fuckin wish I had some. But Canadian Comfort is a rich man's drink, and I'm not a rich man. Anyway, it doesn't matter how bad it tastes. What matters is that when you drink it, it makes Canada beautiful."

"Since you're here," Sal said, "and it looks like you're tryin to get your shit together, I wanna know if you've been workin at all."

Andy shrugged. "Casual stuff. Manual labor. Mainly just workin when I have to, then drinkin and sleepin it off."

"Ever thought of shampooin carpets? That's what

I've been doin. We can always use a helpin hand."

"Maybe. I'll think about it." He thought about Carroll, who would be in bed, probably as restless as he was, each of them thinking about the other. Annie would be thinking about him, too, and fretting about a hundred other trivial things. Carroll didn't worry about something unless she knew it was worth worrying about. Diane worried about whatever her mum worried about, and they all seemed to be worried about Andy. He, for that matter, felt totally unworthy of their concern. Still, he told himself, I put on a hell of a show for them. I showed them what a man can do. A man has balls. He can knock on their door and say hidy.

He looked up and saw a vision of Rikia walk across the room. She smiled and blew him a kiss. Damn ghosts, he thought, they don't have anythin better to do than haunt me.

...

Boylan and Clark entered Mrs. Johnson's flophouse. Then came a third man Andy knew as Stinko.

"Looks like the joint is fillin up," said Andy.

"It's Boylan," said Saskatchewan Sal. "I guess his tent collapsed."

"He's a good sot," said Andy. "He's done me some favors when I really needed them."

Boylan staggered over to them, trying to figure out who they were and why they were talking about him.

"Boylan," said Sal, "how come you're not all nice and comfy in your tent on this cold night?"

"Got no tent." Boylan slurred his words. "All gone now. All burned up."

"But you escaped?" Sal asked.

"I wasn't in it. I went to the store to get some hooch. When I come back, it was on fire."

"Lost everythin, eh?" Sal scratched his whiskers. "Got any idea of who did it? Did you owe anyone some money?"

"Cops did it. I seen them." Boylan staggered off to find a cot.

"He's right," Clark said. "Cops have been bustin up everythin the homeless people have all because of the Games."

"Scumbags," muttered Andy. "Never met a cop

who understood the meanin of 'serve and protect.'"

"We come in here," said Clark, "to get away from the cops."

"You think we're safe in here?" Andy asked.

"Yeah." Clark pointed in the direction of the flophouse's entrance. "We got Mrs. Johnson protectin us."

They all laughed.

"Maybe the cops didn't torch Boylan's tent," said Sal. "Maybe one of the other bums did it. Boylan's got some enemies. He can be a mean son of a bitch."

"You hear that, tough guy?" Andy called over to Boylan, who lay sleeping on a cot. "Sal says we torched your shit because you're a mean son of a bitch. How do you feel about that?"

"Zzzzzz," replied Boylan.

"Boylan's had some hard luck lately," said Clark. "Just leave him alone so he can sleep in peace."

"Yessir, boss," retorted Andy. "Whatever you say, boss."

"Who the fuck are you to talk to me that way?" Clark demanded to know.

"I'm a former Bully who could take you in two minutes."

"Asshole." Clark moved over to Boylan's cot.

"Andy," Stinko said, coming nearer, "as soon as I heard your voice, I thought, 'Andy Kennedy's here tonight!'"

"Stinko," Andy said. "Stinko Kettyls."

"You always had a good memory, Andy. The Cisco hasn't fucked you up yet."

"Speakin of Cisco—"

Kettyls waved him off. "No more drinkin for me. My liver is pickled."

"Then what are you doin here?"

Kettyls gave a little shrugged. "Just came by to say hi, to see who's still alive and who's dead."

"You still friends with Boyland and that little goof Clark?"

"Who you callin a goof?" Clark said as he sat next to Boylan.

"I'm callin you a little goof," Andy said. "You want me to shut up, come over here and make me."

"Lighten up, Andy." Stinko pointed at Andy's

clothes. "How come you're lookin so good? Tell me what you been up to."

"Things are lookin up a bit, I guess. Decent clothes, some booze, money in my pocket."

Stinko nodded. "More power to ya."

"So you're not drinkin, eh? You got a job? What doin?"

"Handyman work out in the suburbs. Got an apartment, a wife and a car. Wanna go for a ride?"

"One of these days."

"How about right now?"

"This guy"—Andy pointed at Stinko as he spoke to Joey—"could drink us both under the table. I saved his life once or twice by callin the ambulance so they could pump his stomach."

Stinko nodded. "He saved my ass, but he's a tough son of a bitch, too. He could take on three guys at once, beat their asses good. I could fight OK myself, but I stopped doin that years ago. Ended up in the hospital, then the nuthouse. Took me quite a while to get my shit together. *Quite* a while." He paused. "So, Andy, how about that drive?"

"Married now, too, eh?" Andy said.

"Married, got a job, apartment and car." Joey shook his head, as if he'd never met such an accomplished individual.

"This is Joey," Andy said. "He wants to jump off the Tyson River Bridge."

Stinko shuddered. "Ooh, that would be cold. Why don't he just drink himself to death? A few bottles of Cisco would kill him a lot faster and funner than drownin in the river."

"I don't want to drown," said Joey. "I'm afraid of water."

Stinko said, "Well if you're feelin so low that you want to end it all, I can understand that. Andy and I once went on a thirty-day drunk and suddenly it was winter. We had no booze, no money, and I went through such severe alcohol withdrawal that I truly wanted to die. Andy here was probably goin through the same thing but he just kept to himself and acted like nothin was wrong. He's the strongest man I've ever met."

After a few minutes of silence, Stinko said, "Now,

how about that ride?"

"I'm goin where Andy's goin," said Joey.

"Well…?" Stinko asked Andy.

"I'm stayin put. "Stinko, why don't you lay them bones on that cot and go to sleep? You must be as weary as the rest of us."

"I told you, I'm on my way home."

"Shut up your gabbin," ordered Clark.

"Make us, goofball," replied Andy.

"Come on, gents," said Stinko. "We better not make trouble, or the old hag who runs this flop will sic the pigs on us."

"Let her call the pigs. I'll punch them out by myself. You said I was the toughest guy around."

"Right now, you're the drunkest guy around."

Andy nodded. "Yeah, I'm drunk and my mind's gone. Wonder where it is."

"It's floating in a bottle of Cisco Berry," Stinko said.

"Gotta hook up with Annie," Andy said. "Maybe she *did* make up with her brother and she's already forgotten about me."

"Annie fanny," said Joey. "Little Orphan Annie granny fanny."

"Joey, shut up," Andy muttered.

Joey pouted. "People say that to me a lot."

"Well, you talk too goddamn much and you never say anythin worth hearin."

"I can't help it, Andy. I'm just bein myself."

"Maybe that's your problem. Try bein someone else for a while. Try bein a deaf mute."

Joey smiled. "I like bein scolded. I feel like someone cares."

"No one's scoldin ya."

"Yeah, you're scoldin, but I like it. Scold me some more. I've been a bad boy and I've done some bad things. I need to be punished."

"You're no worse than anyone else."

"For fuck's sake!" yelled Clark as he sat up and glowered at Andy and Joey.

Andy got up and charged at Clark. He grabbed the chubby little redhead and slapped him in the face. "Want some more? I'm in no mood for your bullshit."

Clark lay back on his cot, rubbing his reddened face

and shaking his head. Andy returned to his cot and looked past Joey, Stinko and Saskatchewan Sal. He saw his mother, Rikia and Carroll standing against the wall, blowing kisses at him. He blinked and they were gone.

"I don't get tough with anyone unless they got it comin," he said to no one in particular. "After I die, and they drop me in that hole, I don't want anyone sayin, 'There lies Andy Kennedy. What an asshole.' There's always been more good in me than bad, and I've helped lots of people without expectin anythin in return. But while I'm alive, I'm damn sure gonna live. I don't understand these bums who are just waitin around to die, who stopped livin long before they stopped breathin. When my time is up and they're buryin me, I want those who cared enough to attend to say, 'Andy was a gentleman to those who deserved it, and he was a tough guy only when bein a gentleman didn't work.'"

"The whole fuckin world," said Stinko, "will mourn you on that day."

Andy shook his head. "No one will give a rat's ass, and there's no reason they should. I know I should stop livin in skid row because I have a family that wants me back. I once had a strong body and sharp mind, but some bad stuff happened and I lost it all. But some of it's still there, my family and home, and I need to be grateful for that."

Stinko nodded. "Too right."

"All alone, and the street's your home," Joey sang out, using a Cisco bottle for a microphone, as he had seen Andy do.

"So," Stinko said, looking at the two men, "nobody wants to go for a ride, eh?"

Andy looked at Joey. "Wanna go? Let's do it."

"See ya," said Saskatchewan Sal as the three men headed for the exit. "Thanks for the Cisco."

"Nothin to it," replied Andy.

"Where we goin?" asked Joey.

"To Waverly and Carlin," replied Andy. "Out by the train station."

"That's where the old Bank of Toronto is," said Stinko.

"They're usin it for other things now," Andy told him. "The bums have taken it over and made themselves at home. I wanna check it out."

"Gonna be cold out there," said Joey.

Andy shook his head. "No, they always got a fire goin."

"Let's do it," said Stinko.

…

As Stinko's car crept through Chinatown en route to the homeless encampment, Andy, for the hundredth time, told himself, *Too bad Chinatown's gone downhill so much. Used to be plenty of fun in the 'Seventies with all that drinkin, dinin and partyin. Thumpin with dance music, glowin with neon signs. Now what's it got? A few borin cafes, a coupla gift shops and lots of boarded-up, padlocked old businesses. But maybe that's what you get for bein located right next to skid row. I hear the Chinatown merchants have to shoo away the bums that's come over to panhandle the tourists.*

"Too bad," he said.

"What?" asked Stinko. Joey, in the back seat, lay in an alcoholic stupor.

"It's just too bad. Chinatown, skid row, this whole part of town. I can remember when it wasn't anythin like this."

"Won't be like this forever. The whole world's fallen in love with Bayporte. Soon the developers will come in and gentrify all of the Lower East End because it's so close to downtown. Then even the poorest part of town will be too expensive for poor people."

...

The Bank of Toronto at Waverly and Carlin had been a handsome stone building identical to a hundred or more B. of. T.s across Canada. Then the bank's top people decided to relocate many of its branches into indoor shopping malls; as soon as they closed the Waverly Street building, homeless people smashed its windows and squatted there. Over time, they customized the facility by punching holes in its walls for more convenient entrances and exits. After the roof partially collapsed, the bums built bonfires inside the bank.

Andy had a friend in the encampment, a man named Francis "Fay" Duwey, nicknamed Fade Away because of his prodigious attempts at drinking himself to death. Andy and Fade Away had traveled together once to the Yukon and stayed friends ever since. Andy looked forward to seeing Fade Away in the encampment, yet he also felt morose and cranky, as he often did after slurping down too much Cisco. He chided himself for slapping Clark in that old woman's flophouse. That was uncalled-for. His current lifestyle, and his recent trip back home, made it clear that he needed his family's love and companionship to sustain him. There *is* something better for you, Andy. All you have to do is go back there and get it.

Stinko parked his car at the curb. Andy climbed out and helped Joey get to his feet. The three entered the encampment and Andy immediately sought out Fade Away.

"Hey! Fade Away! Have a drink." Andy handed a bottle of Cisco to his friend. Fay, always generous with his cigarettes, food and liquor, smiled at Andy, accepted the bottle had took a long drink.

"Andy Kennedy! How's it goin, eh?"

Andy shrugged. "Just takin one breath after another and amazed I'm still alive." Then, "You got room for a couple more? Stinko here isn't stayin long because he's got a job, a wife and a life. Joey here is my best friend. He follows me around like a monkey on my back."

Fade Away laughed. "Always got room for a few more." He pointed to the parking lot, which had become part of the encampment. "As you can see, we've expanded a bit. Isn't it nice how the bank generously donated one of their properties for conversion into low-income housing?"

Andy grinned. "They're just too bloody kind. Must write em a thank-you note sometime."

"Let's go out there," said Fade Away. "It's warmer there because they got a fire goin."

They all went out into the parking lot and sat while Fade Away fed the fire with sticks and cardboard. Soon the flames reached well up into the sky and illuminated the encampment. The men held out their hands, grateful for the fire's warmth.

Andy sensed someone standing behind him. When he turned around, a man stuck out his hand.

"I'm Newton, from Quebec."

Andy shook Newton's hand. "Andy from Bayporte. New in town, are ya?"

"Kind of new. I was squatting in an old house near the harbor till its floor collapsed while I was sleeping."

"Too bad you didn't break your neck," said Andy.

"Who is this guy?" Newton asked Fade Away.

"He's Andy from Bayporte. We've been friends for a long time."

"I don't like his attitude," said Newton.

"Maybe he don't like yours," replied Fade Away.

"I like everyone," said Andy. "I never met a bum I didn't like."

"Who said that?" Joey asked.

"I did, just now."

"Will Rogers said somethin like it years ago," Joey said. "I read it on the computer at the community center. I go there to educate myself."

"Education is a dangerous thing," Andy said.

"What's he babblin about?" Newton asked Andy.

"Just babblin. He likes to hear himself."

"Did you know," Joey said, "that there might be life on Mars? Do you know where Mars is?"

Andy pointed skyward. "One of them shiny little buggers up there."

"Shit I'm hungry," said Newton.

"Got somethin for ya." Fade Away reached into his pocket, withdrew an orange and handed it to Newton.

Newton looked at it, shook his head and handed it back. "No, thanks. It wouldn't come close to fillin me up."

"If you want to eat and drink proper," Andy told him, "maybe you should get a job and draw a paycheck."

"My headhunter's put my resume all over town, but no interviews just yet. I guess they're not hirin for executive positions at the moment."

"You need to stay put," Andy told him. "A rollin stone gathers no moss."

"Well, right now the stone that stays put is gonna be beaten into moss by those boys in blue."

Fade Away said, "The cops came by here earlier tonight, checkin us out. They didn't say boo to us, they just flashed their lights on us for a few minutes and drove away."

Joey looked up at all the faces illuminated by the fire. Then he looked at the huge moon above them and howled.

...

They all drank some more Cisco, and Andy, buzzed again, got up to get some more cardboard for the fire. Within minutes, they had it blazing even hotter. After sitting back down, Andy savored the fire's heat and thought about his visit home.

His son Tom had stood before him, all dressed up.

You like my suit and hat? Tom asked.

Lookin sharp. Lookin good.

I'm not sure about the hat, said Tom. Maybe I should leave it off.

Leave it on, said Andy. It looks good.

OK, said Tom, I gotta be shovin off.

Don't let me keep ya.

I'm lookin forward to your next visit, said Tom.

Me too. You'll hear a knock on the door, and it'll be me.

You going to stay in Bayporte, or what? asked Tom.

For the next while. I have people to see and things to do.

Tell me about it, said Tom.

The two men shook hands and Tom walked out the door. An hour later, as Andy prepared to leave, his daughter Diane squeezed and kissed him so hard he feared she would break his ribs.

Then Carroll said, You must come by again so we can talk.

Yeah, he said. I'll come by so we can talk.

No, she said. I mean really *talk*. There's so much you've missed over the years. It will take a while for us to say the things that need to be said.

Sure, said Andy. I'll be back.

Next time, we can make up a bed on the sofa and you can spend the night.

"Newton," Andy asked, "were you just bullshitin or are you really that hungry?"

"I never bullshit about bein hungry."

"OK." Andy reached into his pocket, took out half a turkey sandwich and handed it to him. "Have a bite or two, but don't eat it all. Remember that there's other hungry folks here, includin me."

"Thankee." Newton took a big bite.

"See what I told ya?" said Fade Away. "Andy here is a stand-up guy."

"You want a bite too?" Andy asked Fade Away.

"No thanks. I'm not starvin. But there's another guy here lookin for food. He's livin in a refrigerator box. He's got a wife and baby."

"They're here now?"

Fade Away nodded.

"Gimme that back." Andy snatched the sandwich out of Newton's hand and found the refrigerator box. He discovered a small fire and a man huddled by it.

"You the guy with a wife and baby?"

"Could be," said the man.

"Well, I got somethin here that you need more than I do." He gave the man the uneaten half of the sandwich plus the remainder of the other one. "Some dessert, too." He handed the man a slice of pumpkin pie wrapped in waxed paper.

The man accepted these gifts with the silent disbelief of someone trapped in the desert who looks up and suddenly feels raindrops on his tongue. Andy disappeared before the man could say thank you, and he rejoined Fade Away's little group by the fire. All of them looked at Andy.

"Gave him a bit of somethin to eat, hey?" asked Fade Away.

"Yeah, since he's got a kid and all. I've eaten lots today. Say, how old is his kid?"

"Don't know. Still a baby."

"Hope his kid lives longer than mine did. My baby daughter drowned while I was givin her a bath. Her mum ever said a word about it to anyone. Can you believe that? A woman doin somethin like that for her man?"

"Sorry to hear about that," said Fade Away.

"Bloody shame," said Newton. "Women are sure somethin, hey? My ex used to turn tricks behind my back but she was always a lady to me. I never knew she was bein unfaithful till I caught her doin a coupla guys at once."

Andy shook his head. "I'm not talkin about some bloody whore. I'm talkin about a woman who lied to everyone to save her man."

"My ex was a cutie, though," said Newton. "You

woulda liked her. She had quite a vivacious way about her."

"Maybe you should introduce us," Andy said.

"Andy won the love of a good woman," Joey said.

"Damn right I did."

"And the love of a good woman," Joey declared, "is second only to the love of a bad woman." He guffawed.

"You've had too much Cisco," Andy said.

"There's no such thing as too much Cisco," Joey shot back. He turned the bottle upside down and let one or two last drops fall into his mouth. "No more Cisco. Whatever shall we do?"

For a moment, all they heard was the crackle of the fire. Then they heard the soft rumble of car engines and the *thwack!* of car doors being opened and closed.

. . .

Andy regretted telling these men about his dead daughter because they had not yet gotten to know him well enough to take him and his tragedies with what he considered adequate seriousness and respect. Andy's confession about his child, made so prematurely, made his loss seem as casual and inconsequential as Joey's blather about Cisco wine and bad women. Andy decided that telling those guys about Elisa showed just how tactless and indiscreet he often was. He concluded that he was as impulsive, stubborn and unwise as any man who had ever lived. He now felt convinced that he would never have the self-restraint or common sense that permitted most men to lead sane, gratifying lives.

Andy had little clue as to how, and why, he differed essentially from those stable, employed men who shared the city with him yet avoided him, and those like him, on the street. He knew he was bigger and stronger than they were, more prone to violence and far less willing to shrug off the minor slights and conflicts of everyday life. He was this way by design, not choice. He supposed he could have stopped himself from slamming that rock into that cop's face, but a comforting voice in his head told him otherwise, and he had to admit it: He had enormously enjoyed bashing that cop and watching him die. But, of course, that was ancient history; why relive it? Also, who could blame Andy for killing Rockin Rod Brollar under that bridge in Detroit? Or what about the bruises on mouthy little Clark or the other men Andy had punched out in ice rinks or other places? His fault, or didn't those guys have it coming?

He knew this: Everything about himself, or at least most things, defied reason or rationality. But that was not to say he could not think for himself. He believed he possessed qualities far greater and nobler than anyone had ever credited him with having. He had his own peculiar logic and moral code that most of his relatives, friends and acquaintances had rarely taken the time and trouble to understand. He had left his parents' home because he considered himself too vulgar for the; he had weakened and punished himself for most of his adult life because he feared his own destructive capacities. *Who* was he? A fighter, yes; a player; a lover. But he was nobody's victim, except, perhaps, his own.

In the heat of the bonfire, Andy closed his eyes and arrived at the deepest conclusion of his life: *My need to right my wrongs is my only constructive work I left to do in this world. Without it, I have no purpose left. I need to live long enough to do this work.*

He looked up and saw a half-dozen Bayporte police officers coming towards them.

. . .

The police entered the encampment without saying anything. They swung their batons at the people's tents, cardboard boxes and other possessions, smashing them into dust.

"Cops!" someone yelled, and everyone scattered.

"What the fuck—?" Joey exclaimed. "Andy—"

"Pigs! Run, dummy!"

"Shouldn't have come here," Stinko said, hurrying over to his car.

Horrified, Andy watched as the police destroyed everything in sight.

"We'd better go," said Fade Away.

"You got anythin here of value?" Andy asked.

Fade Away patted his rump. "Just this."

Andy, Joey and Fade Away formed a huddle in the parking lot. Andy noticed that Stinko's car was gone.

"How come they're doin this? Joey asked.

"Just takin out the trash," said Andy.

The cops had ransacked the building and, the vagrants guessed, would be in the parking lot soon. Andy and the others started moving towards the exit but two cops came up from nowhere and blocked them.

"This one's for me," said a cop, brandishing his baton as he approached Fade Away, who ducked past the stick-wielding peace officer and slipped away into the night. The cop wheeled around and swatted Joey in the back of the head, who cried out and crumpled to the ground. Andy snatched away the cop's baton, smacked him in the mouth with it and, with a pickpocket's finesse, reached down and pulled out the officer's handgun. As the wounded officer went down on one knee and covered his bleeding mouth with both hands, Andy used him as a human shield as he fired two rounds into the other cop, who went down with an almost inaudible thud.

Tossing aside the gun, Andy threw Joey over his shoulder and hurried over towards the harbor. As soon as he reached the darkened, unpoliced streets of skid row, he slipped into an alley and lay Joey on some crates while he closed his eyes and waited for his lungs to stop burning and his heartbeat to slow down a bit. He felt grateful to be away from the cops and trashed encampment but wondered what lay ahead. After a few minutes he picked up Joey and headed back out into the street. He looked in the direction of the encampment and saw flames and smoke.

"They burned it," he muttered. "Burned the whole fuckin thing."

"Who did?" asked Joey in a tiny voice.

"*They* did. Hope all the bums got out in time." Then, "That pig gave you a pretty good crack on the noggin. You feelin all right?"

"No, I got the worst headache of my life. Worse than a Cisco hangover."

"That bad, eh?"

"I can't walk, Andy. Where's Stinko? He's got a car."

"Stinko took off as soon as the fun started. He'd probably stolen that car. He was a car thief for years. He was a lot of things for a lot of years."

Andy put Joey down so he could try to walk, but Joey managed only a step or two and nearly fell over, so Andy slung him over his shoulder again. He started north, towards Saint Peter's, downtown Bayporte's only hospital. He liked Saint Pete's because its staff was used to street people and their peculiar, self-inflicted health problems. Andy didn't relish the long walk to Saint Pete's, but he had run out of options. He had no money for a taxi, and certainly no driver would pick up one homeless man carrying another. Andy hustled past the harbor to the financial district and its towering buildings, staffed by dark-suited guards, that the police seldom bothered to patrol. Andy readjusted his grip on Joey and marched along Vernon Street, a bustling street now in bed for the night, till he reached the venerable old hospital.

"We're here," Andy sang out as he climbed Saint Peter's big concrete steps, thankful that nobody would stare at them or ask many questions. The hospital's emergency room, spacious and well-lit, was where druggies, crazies and profusely bleeding accident victims showed up virtually every day and night.

A nurse hurried over to the two men and helped Andy lay Joey on a gurney.

"What happened to him?" she asked Andy.

"He got conked on the head. He can't walk too good."

"A doctor will see him in a moment. This man is very intoxicated."

"He's got AIDS, too. But right now I'm worried about his head."

The nurse nodded and went away. Andy watched her pick up the phone and start talking. He whispered to Joey, "You still with me, bum? Don't go croakin on me just yet. We got places to go, Cisco to drink."

The nurse stayed on the phone, and Andy was about to go get her, when she hung up and came back to them. She checked Joey's pulse and listened to his chest. "He's gone."

Andy looked at Joey's face and could see no signs of life.

"What was his name?" she asked.

"Hey?"

"His name. What was it?"

"Joey."

"Joey what?"

"Joey Montana," Andy said, thinking of the quarterback he had always admired.

...

It would be in the late afternoon when Andy headed over to the Pattison Hotel to get out of the miserable cold, lay out with Annie on her bed and ponder what he had just been through, what it meant to him, and what, if anything, he ought to do about it. He would walk into the hotel's lobby, wave hello to the desk clerk and bound up the stairs to Annie's room in this third-rate excuse for a lodging establishment with its grime and dreadful odors. He would smile as he saw the sliver of light at the bottom of her doorway, but he would knock anyway because he knew she appreciated such courtesies. When she failed to ask him in, he would open the unlocked door and discoverer her on the floor in her turquoise robe.

He would step inside her room, sit on her bed and spent quite a long time just looking at her. She lay on her back, unsmiling but serene, with her hair fluffy and loose, tumbling about her shoulders. He would tell himself that he often forgot how pretty she could be, mainly because she chose to look ugly.

After staring at her for some time, he would feel tempted to lay her on the bed, but would decide against doing so because she looked too nice just where she was.

He would settle into her overstuffed chair and stare at her some more as the Pattison got louder and busier. Doors slammed and people yelled; cars down below on Waverly Street honked their horns. He would spend so long in that chair, sitting and staring, that he may have dozed off a few times. He couldn't remember, and it didn't matter. He would decide that he had done the right thing in not moving her, because he had never seen her look so tranquil and lovely.

Also, he had not drowned her. Her death was not his fault.

Searching through her suitcase, he would find ticket stubs signed by Wayne Gretzky, Mark Messier and Mike Bossy. Newspaper clippings, too, and a gold-tipped ballpoint pen, and his electric shaver. He would put all these items into his pockets. Opening her closet, he would find her coat hanging there go through its pockets, finding a wad of cash and keeping it, knowing that he would never learn how, or from whom, she had gotten it. He would remember the money he had left for her, and his instructions to Stelfox: *Give her the money, make sure she gets some breakfast, tell her that I'll come by for her or at least I'll be waitin for her at the mission.* Stelfox would get to keep the money. *That's your tip, Stelly. Annie and I thank you.*

He would then sit on the bed some more and continue staring at her, observing her motionlessness. She had her eyes closed, and he thought of all the times he had seen them open, those incandescent blue beauties. His mother and Rikia would levitate above Annie while he sat and pictured her marvelous blue eyes.

It's no use, levitating women would tell him. You can't get any more of her than you've already gotten. She's gone somewhere else now. But he would continue checking her out, and smirk when he noticed, in her suitcase, the Beatles' White Album CD, which she had recently bought, or more likely stolen, and had no hardware to play it. To Annie, music, food, clothing and everything else were more enjoyable when acquired free of charge. Despite shunning popular music, she loved the Fab Four, and Andy would listen as the levitating women sang *Honey Pie* while Annie prepared her soul for departure from her troubled, wasted old body. He would sit there and feel sorry for himself because Annie and Joey had left him to go somewhere infinitely better than Saint Theresa's Mission or the Pattison Hotel. He would tell himself that, wherever they were now, they knew him far, far better than he had ever known them.

Too bad, he would think, that you gotta die before you can get that wise.

Andy would stop looking at Annie long enough to look, literally, at his life as if it were an epic film flickering on the wall. He would fast-forward and rewind it until he found the part where he and Annie lay in each other arms and Annie said, *What I want most is to be buried with the Fenbergs, my own people.* He would promise her that, and tell her he would make sure her headstone said *Annie Alice Fenberg A Beautiful Spirit.*

Andy would remind himself that when beautiful spirits died, evil ones thrived, filling the world with violence, destruction and ugliness. He would tell himself that, despite his own atheism, he should pray for Annie's soul because his prayer, as useless as it might seem to him, was the only thing left for him to do for her. But since his core belief was that churches were just fancy places for pointless rituals where people put their hands together and talked to themselves, Andy asked himself: *What can I do for Annie now?*

He would think about this matter as he sat motionless on her bed and stared some more at her dead body while, outside their room, the world conducted its noisy, indifferent business.

He would want to reach down and stroke her temple, run his fingers through her hair. But no; he knew it would be better to remember touching the live Annie, not the dead one.

Andy would then turn out the light, leave the room and close the door. After saying goodbye to the desk clerk, if the man was still awake, Andy would leave the Pattison Hotel for the last time and reenter the cold, callous night he had come to know so well.

...

By sunrise, he would be huddling in a boxcar as it began to depart eastward, to the Interior Valley. He would have the door mostly closed to prevent the icy wind from getting in, and he would watch, with some disappointment, as the stars, whose heavenly brilliance had so captivated him so many times, faded away in the lightening sky.

Unable to sleep, he would sit and think about what to do next. Which options and choices did he have? None, and neither did anyone else. For the world, and the universe, it seemed to him, made our lives happen a certain way, even—especially—when we had convinced ourselves that we had control over our destinies.

He pictured Elisa in his arms, a warm lump of pink flesh, smiling and gurgling as he beamed at her and spoke of all the wonderful things that awaited her in life. He saw Rikia, Elisa and Annie, all of them mouthing words, and soon the only face left belonged to Rikia, her full pink lips moving until she, too, faded away. He then realized that, after spending years running away from his corpses, he had never escaped any of them. Nor was he meant to.

Johnny Goodtimes climbed in with him, and Andy envied his old friend's spiffy blue suit and gleaming black shoes.

You lookin pretty good, Andy said, for a fella that dropped dead in the woods years ago. How's death treatin ya?

It's all good on the other side, Johnny told him. Didn't expect to see you runnin away again. What's your problem now?

Same problem as before. The pigs are chasin me.

No, said Johnny. No one's after you. You just think they are.

You're shittin me.

I wouldn't lie to you, Andy. The only enemy you have is yourself.

Maybe. Andy took one last drink of Cisco wine and thought, Yeah, this stuff *does* taste like cough medicine.

He also thought Carroll's spare bedroom.

It's a nice place, Johnny said. They have room for you. They even have a bedroom with your name on it.

Yeah, I went there. She wants me back. Andy went to the edge of the car and flung the empty Cisco bottle into the endless brush. He heard music: banjos and harmonicas, sad and sentimental yet somehow uplifting and life-affirming. The moon sank away as the sun rose; the heavenly bodies, like the earthly ones, played their parts, then got out of the way once their jobs were done. Andy decided that *his* job, far from done, needed to be resumed in a small house on Fairview Avenue.

Can you hear that music? he asked Johnny Goodtimes.

No, I can't hear a thing.

I guess you gotta be alive to hear it.

Guess so.

Andy concentrated harder and listened some more. He heard the music even more clearly, and he knew that he didn't have to sleep in the weeds any more or try to kill himself with Cisco wine. He could go right home to where they wanted him, he could eat his wife's cooking and sleep in the same house he'd lived in for years. Once there, he would try hard not to think about the Pattison Hotel, Mrs. Johnson's flophouse or Saint Theresa's Mission. As if he'd never left home, except that he had.

...

"What would you like for lunch?" Carroll asked him.

"Anythin. Ham sandwich would be fine," Andy said.

"Another cup of tea?"

"Lovely." He sat with his back to the window so that nobody would recognize him. He avoided windows throughout the house, and felt the same anxiety now he had anticipated experiencing whenever contemplating this trip home.

"Nobody," Carroll said, "will know you're here. Unless, of course, you want them to know." She encouraged him to read the online news service or at least watch TV. But he had mostly lost interest in the goings-on of the world, and whenever he did pay attention to the news, he usually said to himself, What's that go to do with *me*?

But he wondered, all the time: Would the police ever figure out that he had shot those two officers while that homeless encampment burned? The Bayporte police, as zealous as any law enforcement agency to catch the killers who'd slain their own, would come looking for him, wouldn't they? Or maybe not. The people who knew that Andy had done it—his fellow indigents—wouldn't tell the cops anything.

But if the cops had no idea that Andy Kennedy had stolen one cop's gun and used it to shoot two cops, if they had no clue as to who he was and where to start lookin for him, and to them he was just another wretch who had disappeared from skid row…well, if that was the case, then maybe he and Carroll could start takin walks together around the neighborhood. Maybe walk all the way up Fairview Avenue and really have a look at how the neighborhood had changed.

Yeah, he thought, me and Carroll walkin up the avenue together. That would be fun.